Cover image: Flowering Crabapple Branch

Image sourced from Century Library

Editing by: DerpyWickedFox Editorial

LITTLE DELIGHTS

VOLUME ONE

R. L. RANDOLPH

Sometimes the best cure for a bad mood is reading unhinged, diabolical levels of smut.

Coincidentally, it's also the cure for writer's block.

INFORMATION

This volume contains ten monster romance stories at various spice levels. I wrote them with the intent that they're all set in the same shared world, where non-humans exist alongside humanity.

There is a lot of instant attraction, love, and lust. Each short ends with either an implied happily ever after or happy for now. You never need to worry about surprise pregnancy and some of the character descriptions are intentionally vague to allow you to picture whomever you'd like.

Enjoy!

Starry Eyed:

A woman recovering from grief has her dinner interrupted when two aliens crash land near her home. ***Starry Eyed*** contains very brief mentions of death of a family member (via heart attack) and death of a beloved pet.

Luella (she/her — human), Gahlaght (he/him — alien), and Alruehn (he/him — alien)

Information: double penetration, clit sucker, ridged/flared penis, similar symptoms to heat or rut, emotional manipulation (so light/only if you squint), dominance/power dynamics, fluid kink

Time of the Month:

A human is unable to sleep because of bad period pains, but her vampire partner is determined to help in any way he can.

Claire (she/her — human) and Elric (he/him — vampire)

Information: light daddy kink, fingering, eating out, mild blood play

Night Shift:

During a routine night shift, a human receptionist meets a moth person as they reserve a room for their pollination cycle.

Winifred (she/her — human) and Charlie (they/them — moth person). Charlie's appearance is based on a red tipped clearwing. Winifred has a stutter.

Information: cock pocket & internal genitalia/tentacle-like appendages, sex pollen with mild dubious consent, squirting, anal play

Straight to Voicemail:

A witch interrupts her siren girlfriend just before the work day ends.

Daniela (she/her — witch) and Siobhan (she/her — siren).

Information: power play/dominance and submission, teasing, edging, fingering, eating out, magical strap-on, mommy kink

Strawberry Red:

An overworked human seeks out release at a sex club via impact play taught by an expert, a lion shifter who is familiar with the world of kink.

Ines (she/her — human) and Ellis (he/him — lion shifter)

Information: sex club, rope play/bondage, voyeurism, spanking, introduction to kink, blindfolds, barbed penis, praise, marking/biting

Cure for Loneliness:

A sheltered witch misreads the name of her latest spell, ultimately summoning a demon for the wrong reasons, but they stick around anyway.

Lucy (she/her — witch) and Easohn (they/them — demon)

Information: demisexuality/asexuality spectrum (FMC), no sex, light implied romance

Morning Routine:

An orc-run coffee shop quickly becomes a human's favorite after moving to a new city, but is his friendliness something more, or is she reading too much into things?

Hanna (she/her — human) and Immon (he/him — orc)

Information: mild miscommunication, jealousy/possessive behavior, dominance, fingering, pierced penis, light breeding kink/fluid kink, subspace/aftercare

Between a Knot and a Hard Place:

A human taking a walk at dusk while her vampire partner is busy reunites with an old friend, a werewolf almost in rut that she and her partner both have a lengthy history with. A companion to ***Time of the Month***.

Claire (she/her — human), Harlan (he/him — werewolf), and Elric (he/him — vampire)

Information: shifted sex, open relationship/implied prior consent, knotting & size difference, voyeurism, blood/biting

Unexpected Visitor:

When a human is caught in a freak blizzard, she ends up in a cabin with a yeti, minotaur, and bear shifter until the storm passes. ***Unexpected Visitor*** contains brief mentions of a terrible ex, with implied stalking and the female main character admitting she gives up searching for help while lost in the snow. She is rescued quickly from harm and her ex never appears on page.

Lily (she/her — human), Lawson (he/him — minotaur), Reid (he/him — yeti), and Boone (he/him — bear shifter [polar bear & kodiak])

Information: brief woman in peril, why choose, spitting, blowjobs, size difference, titty fucking, sword crossing (including jerking off together), lots of fluid(s), special penises (knot & bulb)

Assistance Needed:

A vague job listing appears at the perfect time for a human, who soon finds herself running a dragon's entire empire while he slumbers, but what will happen when he awakens?

Maisie (she/her — human) and Reyes (he/him — dragon)

Information: mutual masturbation, magical sex connection,

partially shifted sex, tail play including anal, mid-air fucking, biting

STARRY EYED

"AND AS YOU EXHALE, *remind yourself you are just one speck in the universe. You have no one to please but yourself. You are your world and that is okay.*"

"I am my own world." I exhale the mantra into the night air, though it sounds far different in my southern twang than the woman's crisp British accent. "And that is okay."

The guided meditation clicks off, transitioning into an ad because I can't afford the premium version. Tugging an earbud out, I force close the app, unable to tolerate hearing a commercial when the whole point of the meditation was to feel relaxed and zen. It should be a comforting ritual, not a reminder of what reality actually looks like with bills, capitalism, and bullshit.

Behind me, the house is quiet. I buried Bo last week by his favorite tree out back. He was the best hound — the runt of a hunting litter that some guy was giving away for free down at the gas station. I brought him back to the house just after Nana passed and, for a while, I felt less alone. We got five good years together, but the fresh pain will take double that to fade. He was my only companion left.

Brushing a tear away from my cheek, I clear my throat, turning back to the dark house. Just like Bo, I'll end up living and dying in this same stupid town, only having seen the same four streets, the same hundred people that have lived here, with nothing for anyone to remember me by.

I know other people have grander lives. I've seen it on the news. There's some who didn't even *know* they had monster blood in their family for the longest time. There's others who live in apartments in big cities miles away from West Virginia, with witch neighbors or working for dragon bosses who have hoards of gold. I know there are even non-humans around the state, but everything feels so insular here, like adventure is so far out of reach, it's not even a possibility.

The door creaks as I shut it, dropping my phone and headphones onto the cracked kitchen counter before grabbing my leftovers for dinner. The house still feels homey, partially because I didn't change much after Nana died. I kept all her furniture and just moved from sleeping in the living room to sleeping in her bedroom. Bo slept in there too — she would have hated having a dog in the house, but he was a good boy and I'm convinced she would have warmed up to him.

Taking a bite of my reheated mac and cheese, I nudge around in the fridge with my free hand, pulling out my last soda. Payday is Friday. Tonight feels like a night to rot, where I just want to curl up and watch garbage on my phone — or see if the antenna will pick up something on the TV.

As I crack the tab on the can, the entire house shakes with a *BOOM* that echoes across the valley.

"What the *fuck*." Dropping everything, I turn on a dime, running to the door. Birds scatter from the treetops as I rush outside, a streak of light still in the sky. I follow its trail with wide eyes. Not far away, the trees are smoking, highlighting a scorched area.

I take off across the yard, my blonde hair whipping my face, running directly into the woods and past spooked critters before stopping short. Buried partially in smoldering dirt, a circular ship with a long, thin tail butts up against a copse of trees. The chrome exterior is still fading from the heat of the impact.

There's no visible door, but there's *no way* there isn't someone inside in shock from the crash. I run to the side of it, and after slamming my palms on every panel I can reach, there's a hiss. The side flickers like a hologram before sliding open.

An alien stumbles out, rubbing his head with one hand while two arms brace himself on the edges of the doorway and one arm hangs limp against his side.

"Oh shit," I hiss, reaching for him — *them?* — I don't know. I don't *care* as I help him clamber out, his shirt torn in multiple places, exposing light purple skin mottled with red bruising and micro cuts that leak green blood. He grunts, looking down at me as I guide him over to the base of a tree to sit.

What comes out of his mouth is entirely foreign and garbled. At my baffled look, his hand on his head moves to his neck. After another round of garbled speech, he messes with something, then finally groans, "Understand me now?"

"Yes!" I reach for him, flailing a little at the sight of the bruising healing already, unsure what to do.

He pulls the limp arm closer. "My copilot's still inside. Big green dude, can't miss him."

"Right." I stare at the alien for another heartbeat before turning and running back to the side of the ship. This time I heave myself up and step inside. An insistent beeping echoes through silver halls as I stumble toward what seems like the front of the ship. There I find — just like the other one said — a *big* fucking green dude.

He almost looks like the Hulk, but instead of black hair, his is a darker shade of green compared to his skin, slightly curly at the top of his head. Easing forward a step, I reach for his shoulder, cautious as I peer at his face.

Bright yellow eyes stare back at me as he awkwardly motions to the seatbelt twisted around his torso.

"It's stuck."

This is the weirdest fucking night of my life.

The two of us fumble with the uncooperative seatbelt, before it finally releases with a smack, dropping to the floor. The alien in the seat pushes to stand — he only has two arms compared to the other alien — and casts a confused look down at me.

"Alruehn outside?"

"Is he purple?"

The alien in front of me pauses, then nods. "Yes, he is."

"Then yes, he is outside. Mostly in one piece." I motion him to follow me as we clamber out of the ship only to find the purple guy — Alruehn — standing upright again and flexing the arm that was limp not five minutes ago.

He looks at us, and then at the ship. "This will take a few days to fix."

In the twilight, I can see them both a bit clearer. Alruehn is stacked with muscle, but lean, built more like a runner than a bodybuilder. His light purple skin has a slight shimmer to it that makes me wonder if he's maybe bioluminescent or something — but really I'm just distracted by the sheer amount of fucking arms he's got as he surveys the ship with his head tilted. There's a bit of hair at the top of his head, but it's cropped so close to his scalp, I can't tell the color — not to mention the fact that his eyes are glowing neon green. He's handsome, in a weird purple alien way.

The one next to me waits for a moment before glancing down, his green hair shifting in the breeze. "Sorry about that." As he extends a hand to me, he clears his throat. The spacesuit he has on stretches like a second skin around his bulky form, a few micro tears in it from the crash, but mostly unharmed, unlike the shredded shirt his copilot has on.

Staring at him for a moment, I reach out and take his hand, shaking it slowly. "O-kay...?"

"I'm Gahlaght," the green alien supplies, nodding at Alruehn. "We're bounty hunters. We were headed down here to Earth anyway to find our next job when the ship had a slight... issue."

The two of us look back at the heap of metal just as Alruehn's eyes fade.

"Not as bad as it could be. It'll still probably take a few days for an emergency drone to bring us what we need. I already ordered it." Striding forward, Alruehn grins down at me. "You don't happen to have anyone you want dead, do you, human? Or captured? For bounty?"

My mouth opens as I stare up at him, then I shake my head slowly. "No...? No one comes to mind."

Alruehn frowns. "Damn."

"Wait, what do you mean you ordered supplies?" Holding up my hands at the pair of them, I suck in a ragged breath. "I have a hundred fucking questions and your smoking ship is practically in my side yard."

They exchange a glance before Gahlaght backs away cautiously, tugging Alruehn with him. "We don't mean to overwhelm you. I'm a Yukurian and he's Asparii. We hunt wanted criminals across the galaxy. Earth's been safe for years — right?" He looks at Alruehn, who shrugs and eyes me.

"What's your name? She talks strangely compared to the human that works on the station."

"Luella." Crossing my arms, I frown up at Alruehn. "Don't make fun of my accent."

"*Mai ahkscent?*" He raises an eyebrow at me — well, the skin on his brow moves — there's not actually any hair there.

"Don't mock me!"

"Okay, okay." Gahlaght moves to stand between us. "Maybe our communicator implants are just not used to hearing human speech. We know a human woman — she's mated to the captain of the rig station where we report our bounties."

The information swirls in my head as I just stare at them. "So what happens now? You wait for the supplies that you... ordered in your mind?"

Alruehn blinks. "Well, yeah? I mean Earth is far, but I'd have to be dead not to have my neural connection work. They'll be here in a few days." He flexes the upper set of arms, letting the other pair hang as he glances around. "Is there somewhere we can sleep? Maybe clean up?"

"My house is through there." I point at a set of trees, then feel myself clam up immediately afterward. *Why the fuck would I offer them my house?* There's not a lick of sense left in my body as I stare at Gahlaght.

He dips his chin at me, his expression softening. "We'd really appreciate that. Come on." Grabbing Alruehn's top left arm, he drags the other alien toward the ship. "Let's get our supplies and take *Luella* up on her very kind offer to let us get our bearings on this planet."

Alruehn brushes him off, glancing back at me with a

slightly more salacious smile. "I'll grab a clean shirt so she can't keep staring at my abs."

If anyone asks me about this later, I'll plead temporary insanity because instead of leaving them in the woods to figure their own shit out — I stand there and listen to them bicker through the open doorway to the ship until both aliens emerge with packs on their backs and smiles on their faces. One of Alruehn's set of arms is being used to carry more supplies in silvery bags, but he doesn't seem bothered by it as we tromp back through the woods toward my little house.

At the front door, I hesitate, glancing back at them and the way they just barely miss the frame by ducking their heads.

"Uh..." Flipping on a few lights, I eye the old furniture, the dated wallpaper, and the fact my TV still has rabbit ears from the 80s fixed with electrical tape. "This is... my house." Clearing a few old magazines from the counter, I motion to the two-seater dining room table. "You can set your bags there if you'd like. I... don't know if y'all will fit in the bathroom." Eyeing Alruehn's arms, I frown. "But we can try?"

"Anything is good." Gahlaght smiles. A wash of calm radiates from him, and with it, some of my reservations fade.

After turning on the bathroom lights, I nod at the shower. "I just cleaned yesterday, so take your time. I'll grab the blow-up, I guess?"

Alruehn peers into the bathroom, then looks down at his four arms, tucking the lower pair closer to his body as he steps sideways into the smaller room. "What's a blow-up?"

"A mattress." I can't help but stare as he tears the shred of a shirt off, dropping the remnants into the tiny trashcan next to the toilet before using a hand to fiddle with the shower like he's lived here his entire life. His chest *is* slightly shimmery, like his eyes, and he's so ripped it's like he stepped off of the cover of an 80s romance novel.

"A bed," Gahlaght confirms, nodding his head before he taps the side of his neck. "Sorry, our communicator is struggling with some of the automatic translations."

"Oh." The shower starts behind us and even though I shouldn't, I watch a stark-naked, full purple ass on display Alruehn clamber into my shower, leaving the door open to accommodate his frame as he washes off. My eyes dart up and I turn away before glimpsing his front, focusing on Gahlaght as my cheeks heat.

The green alien in front of me looks around the living room and kitchen, before he pauses, staring at the counter. Bending to look around him, I catch sight of my abandoned dinner.

"We interrupted you." He clears his throat, being careful of the coffee table as he steps around it to get out of my way. "Please, eat. I promise we'll be out of your hair as soon as the parts arrive. If the ship's internal systems hadn't been damaged, we'd stay there. In its current state, none of the routing mechanisms will work."

"I'm... just gonna get you the mattress." Turning around, I jerk open the sliding doors to the hall closet, rummaging past old boxes of Nana's stuff before I find it and the old pump. It makes the *worst* high-pitched squeaking noise when I plug it into the wall, but it's something to do with myself as an alien watches me and another one uses my fucking body wash.

When the mattress is firm to the touch, I unhook the pump and seal the end, looking up in time to see Alruehn standing in the bathroom doorway, a hand towel barely covering whatever he's packing.

Don't think about it.

He smiles, looking down at me. The light bounces off his two sets of canine teeth, giving him the appearance of double fangs.

I bet there's two. Two sets of arms, two sets of fangs, two dicks. Seems logical.

"Shower's yours, Gahlaght." Alruehn strides out, walking past us with his bare ass out again to get to his pack. He bends over slightly and I, once again, look away and catch Gahlaght's gaze flickering between me and his copilot.

"Thank you again for your hospitality." He actually manages to get the door closed partially when he steps into the bathroom, and the moment he does, Alruehn starts snickering.

Shoving up from the floor, I kick the mattress and glare at him. "What is your problem?"

He holds up a single hand, one covering his mouth as he laughs, a pair of... some kind of boxer-type shorts on his lower half. "He's not going to last the night in here with you."

"Sorry?" I tug a spare blanket from the closet, throwing it onto the inflated mattress and then add a pillow for good measure, glancing at the poor couch. There's no way the two of them will lie side by side on the full-sized air mattress — one will have to take the couch, but it's what I've got.

"Listen, I don't need to be from Yuku to sense your emotions around us or *his* after seeing you." Alruehn grins, crossing his lower arms as he nods toward the bathroom. "He's totally smitten. I forget humans are so oblivious. His eyes are *yellow* for fuck's sake."

I hesitate to ask, but it comes out anyway. "Yellow?"

"Yeah, his mood." He waves at his own face. "Yukurians know emotions, can influence them. The sticking point is everyone knows theirs too, because their eyes change."

"And yellow means... love?" My brain shoots back to cheap mood rings I bought as a child that turned my skin as green as the alien we're talking about.

"Arousal." Alruehn does the thing where his brow shifts,

then frowns. “You really *don’t* know anything about us, do you?”

“Only what you’ve said.” Wrapping my arms around myself, I glance anywhere but at him, clearing my throat. The way he says it strokes every inferiority from childhood, not being the best in class, always being a little late, a little dirty because Nana was busy working. “Why? Should I know more? I mean we had the basic classes at school. We know there’s a lot of other people in the galaxy, we sent our own representatives, some of them chose to keep living up there, but also a lot of us don’t have that kind of access — or *money* — and —”

The floor creaks as he walks over, stopping just shy of pressing his chest against mine. He’s really not as tall as Gahlaght, just a handful of inches above me. The extra arms just make him seem bigger than he is.

Alruehn isn’t looking at me when I finally drag my focus back to him. Instead, he’s staring at my house, an even surlier expression on his face. “You’re here alone and you ran to the crash? You helped us out, invited us *home*, and you’re alone?”

“I —” Frowning, I reel back from him. “What’d you want me to do? Ignore the giant spaceship and finish my dinner? I couldn’t do that. I had to make sure you were okay. It’s what good people *do*. They help.”

His mouth dips into a deeper frown. “Do you know anything about Asparii, Luella?”

I don’t even try to pretend like I do. Shaking my head, I frown right back at him. “Sorry I’m not a NASA scientist or whatever —”

“Asparii are known for being warriors,” Alruehn interrupts me, shifting closer. “My planet is full of flora and fauna that can kill me. We grow up, we learn how to protect ourselves, the people we love, and our clan, and some of us move through the galaxy helping others. I *know* about good people. But I also *always* have someone by my side, because it's *stupid* to rush into a situation unarmed, with no idea what's going on —"

"Screw you," I snap back at him, jabbing my finger right in the center of his stupid chest. "Don't you lecture me about what I should or shouldn't be doing in my own damn home. Congratulations on being a big, strong, alien with lots of family and clan or whatever, but some of us don't *have* that —" My voice cuts off in a little hiccup and I turn sharply, my jaw tightening. "Enjoy the couch. Or the mattress. I'm going to bed."

Stomping around him, I head toward the hall just as the bathroom door opens and Gahlaght looks out, his expression pained and his eyes a deep purple. Looking away sharply, I slam my bedroom door shut behind me, refusing to acknowledge the two big, dumb aliens in my living room.

Nana would have a whole second heart attack if she was still here.

You try to help people and not a single thanks. With a little snarl, I rip the covers back on my bed before kicking off my shoes and clambering under the blankets. Twisting this way and that, I punch my pillow once for good measure then collapse onto it, staring into the dark.

My stomach grumbles as I hear footsteps only a few feet away. The walls are pretty thin, but the conversation trickling through them is in another language. Stupid alien communicators.

The sound of the pair conversing lulls me into a gentle state of half-coherent rest. I know they're there, but it's not like I'm afraid of them. Bounty hunters are known all across the world and galaxy. They're registered with the International Space Alliance. If I really wanted to, I could take the time to call the help line and verify their story — but it's not worth it. It's not like people are rushing to impersonate bounty hunters. Their job sucks. It turns out half the people on earth, the monsters that live with us, and the aliens across space produce their own fair amount of crappy people. Sometimes those people have to be tracked down and turned into the proper authorities.

One of them turns on the kitchen sink and I roll over, screwing my eyes shut as I try to ignore them. After a moment, it seems to work. They aren't talking, the noise of the house settling turns into the normal sounds of the forest outside, and I can *almost* forget everything that's happened.

Until there's a little grunt.

Suddenly, I'm not as sleepy as I was a few seconds ago. My ears strain, listening intently as someone exhales harshly. One of them says something in a guttural language that sends a shiver up my spine. The sounds continue, soft, but audible, until I slip out of bed and stop at the door. Everything in this house is old, and while I can avoid some of the floorboards that make the most noise, both of them will know immediately when the door opens more than a sliver.

I chance it when I hear another, longer groan.

The slip of a view I allow myself is enough to see down the short hallway. Half of the couch and the bottom half of the air mattress are just visible. I can only see part of Gahlaght, mostly his green back as he sits on the mattress. But I can see Alruehn clearly. Two of his hands are behind his head as he lounges, thighs splayed, while the other two hands busy themselves in his lap.

I was right.

His two cocks bob, a darker purple than his skin, flushed and leaking on his hands as he strokes them both. The bottom one is significantly larger than the top, the girth double of the upper. Both of them look relatively similar to a human man, including a single pair of balls hanging under them. It could be normal — save for the fact there's two and they're purple.

Though he does look like he's leaking *quite* a bit on himself as he strokes them.

He grunts, one thumb skirting over the head of his lower cock to spread his arousal as he stares at Gahlaght.

I watch as green shoulders heave. Gahlaght breathes heavily, the source of the noise from earlier, as he makes little whimpering sounds. "Hurts. Need to come."

"So come." Alruehn teases himself, smiling at the other alien. "You'll feel better. You always do."

Gahlaght sucks in a breath before it shudders out of him with another little whine. I stare as he shifts slightly, then stretches a leg out. It's the perfect angle for me to see his hand moving along the cock between his legs, one hand jerking it rapidly, running over hard ridges as the other palms something above it. Unlike Alruehn, he has no external balls, just smooth skin.

His head tilts back and I feel a flush of arousal as I watch, transfixed. His palm moves away from his pelvis, but it's almost slow, like his skin is stuck for a moment. Then the ridges on his cock flare, before he curses in a language I don't know. A dribble of cum spurts from the tip, dripping down the length of him as he sighs and leans back on the air mattress, hanging his head.

"It's not enough... not good enough." He lets out a broken sigh, hand still moving on himself.

When I look back at Alruehn, his green eyes are on *me*. His hands move steadily as he tips his chin down, giving me a daring look full of so many unspoken questions. Am I just watching? Am I going to step out and *help* since I was so adamant that's what good people do? Desire swirls in my stomach at the challenge. It's an offer I can't refuse with how flushed I feel all over just from watching them both.

The door squeaks as I pull it all the way open and pad

down the hall, lingering just outside the living room. Gahlaght looks up, his throat bobbing as his cheeks flush green, lips parting. "Lu — I —"

It's a little pathetic how much it makes my stomach lurch with desire to see him so undone, whimpering and shaking as he fists himself. Sinking down to my knees on the air mattress, I watch as his other hand rubs across his pelvis again, my lips parting as his palm moves away to expose a small ridge that's vibrating and sucking at the air.

If I was fucking him, it would line up perfectly with my clit.

"What do you need?" I hesitate before my hand slides over his shoulder, ignoring the fact that Alruehn is watching everything. Gahlaght stares at me, eyes bright yellow, his nostrils flaring as he moves his hands away from himself.

"Nothing. I should... mind my manners." He swallows hard and I catch his hands twitching.

"A little late for that." With a smile, I shift to tug my old t-shirt over my head before slipping out of the ratty shorts I've had on all night. In just my underwear, I move closer, running my hand down Gahlaght's shoulder, then across his chest. "Be honest with me." Leaning in, I brush my lips across his cheek experimentally, my voice softer. "What am I feeling?"

He moans, turning his head so our noses touch. "Want."

Nodding, I slide into his lap, settling there as I cup his face and kiss him slowly but surely. The couch shifts with movement, but Alruehn says nothing as Gahlaght's hands map over my back, skirting around to brush across my full breasts. He explores me with gentle touch, like he's almost afraid this isn't real. The kiss is slow, heavy as he rolls his hips up against my underwear, breathing hard against my lips.

"If she wants you, you should have her." Alruehn's voice makes me shiver. I pull back slightly and look over at him. His hands move lazily, more toying with himself than providing any kind of actual stimulation, though his other set has moved from behind his head, bracing on the sagging sofa.

Under me, Gahlaght lets out a little whine as he ruts up against my underwear. "Is that okay, Luella?"

His desperation makes me feel a little feral. Pushing his hair from his forehead, I murmur, "You want my pussy, Gahlaght? Would that make you feel better?"

His lips land on my throat as his hands move to grasp at my hips. "I would be honored to feel you. I don't take this lightly or for granted." With a little grunt, his head rears back when I reach down to slip out of my underwear, leaving myself open for him as I resettle on his lap. Casting a glance at Alruehn, our eyes lock as the hand on his upper cock starts to move a little faster.

I grind down against Gahlaght, arching my back as we both moan. The ridge at the front of his pelvis seems to shudder with excitement as he lifts me carefully, lining up with me before he whispers, "Thank you."

His hands tug me down, breaching me without another word. The intense pressure of his cock slamming into me takes my breath away, but there's no pain, just indescribable pleasure as the ridges along him shiver inside me, flaring as he moans low and deep. Spasming around him on instinct, I gasp when the ridge above his pelvis lines up with my clit, sucking at it before suctioning me down on top of him and sealing us together.

"Oh *fuck*." Grabbing Gahlaght by the hair, I grind against him as he pants and shakes. It's not really a thrust, more a rock as his cock stays buried inside of me, warm and heavy. The ridges on him roll like a massager, stimulating my inner walls and I gasp when my clit pulses from pleasure.

His breath is hot on my cheek as he holds onto my hips, moving us together. When he whines, it fills the air with the sounds of his overstimulated indulgence. It's music to my ears. *I'm* doing this. I'm making him feel this good, this satisfied.

"Is she good?" Alruehn whispers from behind me. "I bet she's tight and wet, the perfect hole for you to bury inside. Savor her." Clinging to Gahlaght's hair, I tip my head back to watch as Alruehn's hands move over his cocks. His grin drips with desire as he licks his lips. "Yukurians are known for their love of pleasure, no better emotion to lose yourself in, right Gahlaght? He's never been able to take me though, even though we've tried time and time again. He doesn't really have a hole big enough, even his jaw gets tired trying to suck me off, but you could do it, couldn't you, Luella? Just like you're taking him nice and deep, now? Are his ridges catching on the walls of your cunt yet? Vibrating from the inside so your pleasure can feed into his?"

Gahlaght almost sounds drunk as he mumbles and ruts up into me, the sucking getting even more intense on my clit as I spasm around him. He whines, hands on my ass as he suddenly puts me on my back, bending over me with my legs around his waist, pushing deeper. The angle change makes my eyes cross as the rhythm of the ridges on his cock speed up. They *are* vibrating inside me, a rolling pleasure that makes my toes curl as his pelvis latches onto my clit, like it knows I'm going to come.

"You *are* coming," Gahlaght gasps, slurring his words as he looks down at me. His eyes glow in the dark, bright yellow like sunlight as his shoulders shake. "Cover me, Luella. Soak me so I can remember this decades from now and get high off the memory of your cunt."

Arching off the air mattress, it shakes under us as I let out a little scream, tightening around him, but feeling stretched as the ridges flare again, pushing and pushing against my inner walls as my clit pulses. I come with a cry of surprise, my hands dropping to the blanket under us as my entire body shakes with the orgasm.

Above me, Gahlaght shouts and I feel the way the ridges flutter when he floods me with cum. The sucker on my clit pulses before releasing from me and he slips free with a gush. Compared to the little cum that came out from his own hand, I'm dripping with it. I breathe out hard, staring up at the alien above me as he collapses to the air mattress, rolling onto his side with a dumb look on his face.

"He's high," Alruehn supplies from the couch.

Turning to rest my cheek on the bed, I stare at Alruehn's hands as they move over himself. His lips purse as he breathes a little harder.

"He refuses to take a pleasure bot with us. We go through this every fucking time he finds someone attractive, but there's never any release so he gets the full effect. Asparii mate for life. He gets weird about using bots or companion companies. We've been copilots for a while."

I slide my hand down, running it between my thighs and circling my sore clit with a finger. It makes me jolt, but there's a hum of arousal still there as I flick it softly and watch Alruehn stroke himself.

"What about you?" My voice comes out huskier from screaming. Light desire rolls over my skin at the thought of the two of them traversing the galaxy, of Alruehn pushing Gahlaght to pleasure himself while they sit across from each other. The concept has me breathing fast again in no time at all.

Alruehn flexes his upper set of arms as he slides lower on the couch. "Takes a while for me to come." He pants, choking his lower cock so hard his purple skin stretches white across his knuckles. "Feel free to try and make it faster."

Even though I'm dripping with Gahlaght's cum and can

still feel the impression of his ridges inside me, I push up, stumbling two steps to the couch. Alruehn's upper arms catch me around the waist, pulling me inches from his hands on his cocks as my legs spread. He looks down, licking his lips before sliding two fingers into me without warning. I moan, feeling myself tense before they stroke in and out a couple times. Pulling the hand away, he lifts it to his face, sucking the two fingers into his mouth with a toothy smile. "You and him taste good. I'll clean you up after I'm done."

As he starts to lower me, I grab onto one of his forearms. "Wait—"

Alruehn freezes, his arms shaking as they hold me up.

"I can't take you." I stare down at the thick lower cock, his head weeping but aimed straight for my ass.

He grunts before flipping me around like a doll, putting my back to his chest. As he bends down to my ear, he lowers my hips a little more, rubbing his cocks through the combination of mine and Gahlaght's cum. "I forgot. You can do it this way, can't you?" His upper cock nudges against my ass, and I exhale as the purple head of it teases the ring of muscle.

"Maybe," I admit, leaning against him as his lower cock grows slick with all the fluids between us. Alruehn reaches a hand down, running it over my stomach, pudge visible. It doesn't seem to bother him, and it certainly doesn't bother me when he hooks two fingers in my cunt again and stretches me, sliding the tip of his larger cock into me. I shiver as I moan, sinking down onto him as his fingers slip free.

His breath heats the back of my head as he seats himself inside me. Alruehn pauses, and I can hear the grin in his voice when he stills. "Just as fucking tight as I knew you would be, you can barely take just this one. I'm going to split you in two when I take both your holes."

I groan as I push against him, fluttering my muscles over

him. It does the trick and he grunts, pushing in deeper. Dropping a hand, I grab one of his free ones and make him touch my clit, giving him all my weight as I lean back into his chest. Then I guide another hand to play with my nipples, my eyes rolling into the back of my head.

"Shut up and fuck me."

He growls, but goes quiet save for panting as he works himself inside me. One of his lower hands moves, grasping his upper cock just to stroke it and press it harder against my ass. I try to relax, but it only happens once his fingers begin to massage my clit in tight, quick circles. Desperation to feel the fullness of all of him makes me writhe as Alruehn thrusts up just as I grind down. His upper cock finally breaches my ass, sinking into me as his thicker, lower cock pulses inside me.

We both moan, echoing one another as my eyes find Gahlaght.

He sits on the edge of the air mattress, toying with the ridge at the front of his pelvis with a blissed-out look on his face. "You look so good full of him, Luella, dripping with me. He's so big it pushed right out of you. I can come *so* much for you."

Behind me, Alruehn moves deeper, then slides out again. A slick, sucking sound emits between us as he starts to thrust at a steady pace, moving me over him like I weigh nothing. All four of his arms work in tandem — two holding me with hands on my waist, while one rubs my clit and the other keeps my cheeks spread.

Gahlaght sighs happily, playing with himself as he watches. "We should keep you."

A flash of desire strikes through me as Alruehn echoes the sentiment behind me. "Want to come with us, Luella? We'd be so good to you, just the three of us and the stars."

The idea of speeding through galaxies with them takes my

breath away. Throwing my head back, I let out a moan as Alruehn works me back up to the crest of an orgasm. His upper cock slips in and out of my ass, keeping me open and wanting more as his lower strokes every inch inside of me. He's right, he fills me so well it's almost too much, but the pleasure building doesn't care. *I* don't care as long as he doesn't stop.

Hands land on my open thighs and I look down in shock as Gahlaght kneels between Alruehn's spread legs, staring up at us with a reverent expression.

"Say yes."

I moan as he bends down, licking my clit with his tongue as Alruehn's hand fists his hair and holds him against us. With each thrust, it fucks us against Gahlaght's face. He looks thrilled by it, pressing closer as Alruehn shivers behind me.

"I..." I hiccup, turning my head to stare at Alruehn over my shoulder.

His green eyes are dark, hooded as he leans forward, capturing my lips while his last hand moves to cup my head. "Don't answer now, just come for us."

It's the permission I needed. I shake in his arms, stars bursting behind my eyes as Gahlaght's tongue moves over me and Alruehn lets out a broken moan against my lips. The first cock to explode is the one in my ass and wetness slicks between my cheeks, rolling to join the rest of the mess between my thighs. His lower cock buries inside of me as he comes. I feel it jerk multiple times, losing count as I shiver in his grasp.

When I come to, Gahlaght licks my thigh. Alruehn tugs him by the hair away from me, then slides free, immediately replacing himself with a hand between my legs to hold everything in place. I gasp as he lifts me with his lower limbs until I'm level with his head, only then does he dive in, moving his hand so he can suck and lick up every drop leaking out of me.

My entire body goes limp as he holds me. Gahlaght's needy

hands run up and down my upper body, prolonging the over-stimulation and post-orgasm high. I sink into them both, visions of what they just asked playing out in my mind — adventures on other planets, nights spent on the ship between them — the concept of it all is so lovely, it's like my mind floats away in the bliss.

I wake up in the morning swaddled in blankets on the deflated air mattress. Sizzling emits from the kitchen as I come to, my throat dry and body spent.

Gahlaght looks more alert than ever, practically bouncing as his eyes flash pink. His big green body moves from side to side, pulling plates down from my cabinets as Alruehn juggles three pans on my four-burner stove. The two aliens work around each other with smiles until Gahlaght looks over.

I swear to god, hearts burst in his pink eyes as he comes over, cupping my face to kiss me deeply. Leaning into him, I laugh, half-breathless when he pulls back.

"We made breakfast."

Blinking, I look past him to Alruehn as he plates eggs, toast, and bacon. I have no idea where they got any of it — my fridge was bare as of last night, but I don't question it. Instead, I pull Gahlaght closer and press my cheek to his. One of his arms wraps around me as the blanket dips, exposing my skin to the cool air.

"Yes."

He freezes, then moves my face so he can stare at me. "Yes?"

I bite my lower lip, then nod. Gahlaght's eyes turn blue, then pink, then yellow, so rapid it's a blur of color before I lift my head to stare at Alruehn. "Yes."

He puts all the pans down and walks over slowly before sinking to kneel next to the air mattress. One set of his hands pulls us both to him, while the other set wraps around my waist. I melt into the pair of them, smiling as I kiss them both at the same time, whispering, "Yes, you can keep me. Yes, I'll go with you. Let's fix the ship and leave."

Gahlaght's delighted laugh fills the air. "We're keeping you. And you can keep us."

Alruehn's lips touch my jaw. The warmth radiating from Alruehn makes my heart flutter as he nods. "Breakfast first, Luella. Then we'll explore the galaxy together."

TIME OF THE MONTH

"Darling? Are you alright?"

The bed stretches between us, a warm and plush void that Elric breaks by wrapping long arms around me and pulling me into his cool chest. Normally, I'd melt into the way his skin holds no warmth of its own, but tonight I'm already chilled with two blankets on and the thickest pajamas I own.

"I'm cold," I mutter into the curve of his collarbone. "And cramping. And emotional." Sucking my bottom lip between my teeth, I wrap my arms around him as I worry with it. "But my period is late and all the symptoms just keep getting *worse*."

He makes an affectionate sound as one of his hands raises, stroking over the back of my head. "Sweet Claire, I'm sorry." His lips are the only warm thing about him as he kisses my temple, running hands over my head, neck, and down my back before tugging me closer and tucking the blankets around us firmly.

I know I've been fidgeting too much if my vampire has noticed the disturbance. He's supposed to be dead to the world from sun-up to sundown. Even though there isn't a whisper of light escaping into our room around the blackout shutters, my body senses it's still not time for either of us to be awake.

"I'm sorry you're dating a human with hormonal issues."

"I'm not." The words are a whisper as his head shifts, then his lips brush mine, featherlight and gentle as he continues to speak. "I love you dearly. From the sheer fact you changed your sleeping routine to accommodate mine to the way I get the pleasure of listening to your steady heartbeat beside me in bed."

My stomach flutters as I kiss him back, smiling against his lips. "You're so smitten."

"Mm." Elric makes a noise of agreement before sliding away briefly. Muted orange light casts over the bed from the dimmable lamp on his nightstand. It's enough of a glow for my eyes to adjust, watching as his pale, shirtless body crawls toward me. Lithe muscle cords through his upper body, leading to defined shoulders, a regal jawline, full lips, Aquiline nose, and sharp red eyes.

His dark blond hair flops onto his forehead as he reaches for me, guiding me back to the bed with gentle hands. After adjusting the pillow just so to support my neck, Elric drops a kiss to my pulse-point with a tiny smile.

"I must admit," he says against the skin of my throat as his fingers pull the neckline of my sweatshirt down to expose more of me to him. "It baffles me how you tolerate this *every* month. The hormonal changes. The bodily discomfort. You're far stronger than I would be in your situation. I can always smell when it's close, but I do hate when you have this many symptoms to contend with."

I can't formulate a response as his hands push at the hem, cool fingers pressing against my swollen and bloated stomach and easing the pain for a moment as he massages me gently.

After soothing me with his touch alone, Elric's fingers play over the band of my leggings, pausing.

"These are digging into you."

Barely lifting my head off the pillow, I look down, unable to see anything past my chest in the oversized sweatshirt.

"I told you, I was cold when we got into bed —"

They rip like tissue paper in his hands, cutting me off with a gasp as the cool air of the bedroom coasts over my bare skin. This time I *do* sit up, staring down at Elric as he tosses the offending fabric to the floor, kneeling between my legs with a self-assured smile, his tongue curling around a fang.

"How useless. They're so thin they just came right off. I must buy you a better pair."

In a flash, his hands are around my bare thighs, dragging me down to the bed under him. He kisses the exposed skin and I dissolve into giggles, wiggling under him as he effortlessly keeps me mostly in place. There's no doubt he's strong enough to make me stay put, but there has never been one time in our relationship where I've feared the monster holding me down.

"I am over seven *hundred* years old and yet I've never seen more perfect" — Elric grabs my thighs, palms full of flesh as he groans — "thighs than yours. You're decadent." He bends closer, suckling on the soft skin before moaning. "So lush." His fangs graze me and I shiver for an entirely different reason as his tongue darts out to run over his favorite artery, covered by a layer of fat and skin.

Dropping back to the pillow, I fist some of his blond hair in my hand, moaning and arching into his mouth. "Pretty words and compliments only go so far, El."

He presses another kiss to my thigh, running his tongue over my pulse once more before sighing and turning his head. With his cheek resting on me, his red eyes find mine, hooded and dangerous.

I could stay by his side for eternity and never tire of the way he looks at me.

"What would make you feel the best tonight, darling? My hands?" He toys with the edge of my underwear, running a slender finger over the damp gusset. "Would you like my fingers deep in your cunt, coaxing out a nice orgasm to make your cramps abate while my tongue is on your clit?"

My heart stutters. His lips twitch at the sound. "Yes? Does that sound good to you, little pet? I promise —" Elric tugs my underwear to the side, inhaling deeply as he presses closer to my core. "Daddy will make you forget all about your monthly nuisance."

Another shiver works its way up my spine and I feel half flushed and feverish as I make a pathetic little sound when his lips encircle my clit, kissing it as gently as he kisses my mouth.

"Please, daddy." My fingers relax in his hair, a slight tremor in my touch as he hums, sending a jolt through my clit and striking the rest of my body with a vibration of aftershocks. It's all the permission he needs to reattach his lips to my clit, sucking on it as he rips away the barrier of my underwear to expose me to him.

Suddenly the room doesn't at all feel cold anymore, and neither does he. Elric's fingers part me as I whine, making low noises as he spreads the arousal already threatening to drip out of me. I've never felt so fucking turned on in my entire life as his thumb teases my entrance, thicker than the rest of his fingers and adding an element of drag as he hungrily laps at every inch of my pussy.

"Ah —" I suck in a tiny gasp, hiccuping out a soft "*Daddy!*" when his thumb finally breaches, slipping into my cunt just as his tongue flickers across my clit rapidly, so fast it's like a vibrator on the highest setting. In seconds, my muscles lock and I come with a squeak, pressing his head against me as his thumb thrusts in and out in shallow strokes, a barely-there tease compared to the overstimulation of his tongue.

Elric pulls back just enough to chuckle, nipping at my swollen cunt, careful of his fangs. "Look at this sweet pussy, all flushed and wet for me." Kissing the top of my mound, he licks his lips, watching his thumb move in and out as the first orgasm sizzles through me and fades, leaving a slow heat behind.

"I do think you have at least one more in you."

A deep cramp makes me groan as his thumb slides free, taking the pleasurable distraction away. Elric sucks it into his mouth before lifting my thighs, bracing each on a shoulder and bending down to thrust his tongue into me. I choke on the feeling, a syrupy haze of bliss settling over my bones as he nudges my clit with his nose, keeping a practiced rhythm going that has my legs shaking and toes curling in no time.

"D-daddy —" Fire licks up my spine, igniting the pleasure like kerosene. Tension coils in every muscle, making my jaw shake as I try to get anything coherent to come out of my mouth, reduced to just gasping, "Daddy, please, oh — fuck — I —"

The last thing I hear is his laugh, gleefully evil as the orgasm hits me hard enough that I lose my senses for a moment. Writhing against his hold on the bed, I scream as I tighten around his tongue, certain his fingers holding my thighs open will leave bruises.

With a shaking breath, I sink back into the pillow, twitching as Elric's tongue continues to lap at me. My toes curl, then uncurl, then curl again as he groans, pushing closer. It's only when I feel his fangs pressed against me that I let out a soft moan, tugging on his hair.

"I'm sorry, pet." Elric finally drags himself up, kissing me slowly as he slides a hand around to cup the back of my neck.

"You just taste so good on the first day. I'll run you a warm bath." His lips trail over my jaw as he lifts me gently from the bed. "And make you a very bloody steak so your iron count doesn't dip too low."

He's right — the cramping eases, and instead I just feel a dull ache in my body as my head lolls onto his shoulder. Reaching down, I press my fingers against myself, pulling them away to find them wet with arousal and blood. I laugh incredulously, turning to kiss his shoulder. "You made me come so hard I started my period?"

"Yes." Elric grins down at me, flashing me his wickedly sharp fangs. "I did."

NIGHT SHIFT

THE MOTEL'S vacancy sign flickers, emitting a soft buzz as I flip open my book. The paperback is so old that the pages give a threatening crinkle that they may rip, but I don't care — it's some yellowed romance novel I found at the thrift store a few weeks ago and threw in my bag for nights like this; evenings when the rooms are mostly full and I need a distraction from the night shift.

We're not the most popular motel in the south, but we get enough foot traffic being a few miles off the highway to provide a level of discretion for visitors. I don't even know who owns the place, just the manager — Jeff — who pays me every couple weeks to keep the office lights on and make sure any complaints are handled.

Our clientele doesn't often file complaints.

The few humans who walk through the door know what they're getting into. The motel's primary clients are the monsters, the unique Others, ranging from vampires appearing in a flash just after sunset to a very kind Minotaur who seemed a little embarrassed when I explained the included cleaning fee required for her stay.

Our motel is a mere stopping point for those with mating cycles.

I'm not familiar with how it works in cities. Hotels in rural areas aren't exactly equipped to host a centaur one night and a minotaur the next, but a select few motels have been converted over the years. We boast rooms for all types of people, with a wide range of selections. They even closed off the old pool and made it into a private space for the rare sea creature who needs it. Though I've never met one — they seem to stick to the coasts, not land-locked Tennessee.

Jeff is human, as far as I know. I have a theory that the people who own this place aren't, but it's probably easier to employ a human to oversee things than someone who has a whole mating cycle of their own to contend with. It's definitely bad for business to have your workers screwing around — literally — on the job.

My eyes glaze over a little as I stare down at the paperback, lost in every thought but the words on the page. Two night shifts back to back isn't bad, but three? Four? Everything starts to blur together.

The tiny front office and lobby consist of my desk, faded wallpaper, and a single loveseat that's slumping in the middle. I don't know when the frame broke, but it's barely a usable piece of furniture anymore.

Shutting the book, I lean back in the office chair and let out a sigh. We used to have all these pamphlets for everyone who might check in. Trifold printer paper emblazoned with tips for your stay, features of the various types of rooms, and equipment the guests could request. They phased those out pretty soon after I started working here at eighteen. Now, years later, I just take a payment and toss them a key. What happens in the room is *not* covered by my minimum wage pay.

The bell above the door makes a half-hearted clank as someone pushes it open. Blinking, I feel my lips part in shock as they step inside the tiny space, wings held as close as possible to their frame. They're easily over seven feet, maybe eight? And with their head tucked down, I can't see much of their features, but the moth person carefully shuts the door behind themselves, black feathered cowl around their neck rustling nervously as their wings flutter.

The glimpse it gives me makes my breath stop. Their wings, even tucked close, are jet black with *crimson* around the edges. But it's not just that, they're not full-feathered; they're some kind of glossy, shimmering translucence hanging behind them, almost like a fairy from old children's books.

I've never seen someone so beautiful.

Shuffling forward, the moth person adjusts their head, giving me a glimpse of a strong brow and thin, tight lips as they look down at me in the little chair. Their nose is flat to their face, and they have no hair, just feathers laid flat around their antennae. Their body is mostly covered by a large trench coat, the kind with slots in the back for winged individuals.

"One room."

"Y-Yes, sure." I flail for a moment, turning to the ancient computer in front of me to check that there's a vacancy with double-height ceilings. Their voice echoes in my mind, not melodic or chirping, but deep and monotone, a command not a request.

After confirming availability, I hunt down the key in the drawer and then peer up at them again. "Would you like our hourly or nightly rate? If you p-pick nightly there's a slight d-dis —" I cut myself off, biting my tongue.

This is why I've never worked another fucking job. Jeff just keeps me around because there aren't many monsters who come by when I'm on shift.

Closing my eyes, I blow out a slow breath. "Discount."

"Nightly, please." Their voice softens, not as monotone as before as I focus on the screen, filling out their information after they slide me an ID. *Charlie Clearwing* stares back at me from their photo, their gender marker confirming what I'm used to. Most moth people don't adhere to human gender norms, I'm not sure why — other than the obvious being that it's not like any Insectoid or Arachnae technically *have* a defined sexes biologically. Some of them are even entirely self-reproducing.

"Thank y-you." I try my best to flash them a customer-service friendly smile, sliding their ID and key across the desk-top. "Room num-num-nuh —" I suck on my teeth, redirecting to point to the number thirteen on their key tag, forcing out a soft, "Enjoy."

They tilt their head at me, wings rustling as they reach out for the items. Their hand is very similar to a human's, albeit black feathers start on their forearms, soft, downy, and smaller than the ones around their cowl.

"Thank you, Winifred." Charlie makes sure to catch my eyes as they look up from the name tag on my chest, their thin lips lifting in a gentle smile before they turn and leave through the front door.

The bell clanks as the front office returns to silence broken by the occasional buzz of the sign outside. Rubbing my jaw, I turn back to the computer, checking the availability before toggling the digital sign from vacancy to no vacancy. We've had that same minotaur in one of the other large rooms for damn near a week and I don't envy her because I've heard ruts are a nightmare to get through.

Not that I know a lot of non-humans — but she's barely

shown her face outside of her room barring getting food deliveries and a small kerfuffle when I had to... escort her gentleman caller to the door because he got turned around.

My face and throat feel tight as I finish filling out the necessary information for the last guest, leaving what Jeff will need when he bothers to show up in the morning. As I try to slow my breathing and remind myself that the stutter is normal, that *I'm* normal for having trouble sometimes, I inhale and then immediately sneeze.

It rocks through my body, sending me back in the office chair as I look up in alarm. There's a light cloud of glitter in the air. A shimmering sheen that makes me blink slowly as I reach up and wave my hand through it. The dust is so fine it doesn't even look real for a moment. Leaning up, I pull my hand back and examine the way the dust settles on my skin, a light pink luminance left where it touches.

As I breathe in again, the dust surges forward, almost like it has a mind of its own. Instead of sneezing this time, I feel a little woozy as it invades my mouth and nose. Blinking rapidly, I touch the desk, bracing myself as I glance at the windows. Maybe I should open one? The other moth people I've checked in have never left this substance but I've never seen one like *Charlie*.

The thought of them makes my head spin, my heart pounding in my chest. A flush of heat drips down my spine like sweat on a hot summer day and I pull at the collar of my sweater.

The sign has no vacancy. They're in their room. I could just... go ask what this is.

I wouldn't want to clean it up if it's important to them.

Before I know it, my hand is on the door leading outside. Wavering for a moment, I look back at the desk, trying to reconcile the fact I don't really remember walking over here.

The next time I blink, I'm staring at the door for room thirteen.

"What—"

My hand jiggles the knob and I look down at my own limb like it's not even attached to me. I stop, forcing myself to take a step back as I breathe in and out deeply, looking around the line of doors making up this section of the motel. The open air helps for a moment as my brain spins, trying to understand how I got from the office to here.

The door in front of me opens a crack. It's enough for another puff of the pink powder to hit me right in the face.

Instead of coughing, I feel electrified. Staring up at the sliver of Charlie I can see, I feel my mouth drop open.

"Ah, shit." Their voice is muffled by the door as they shift and then open it a little more. "Come here." They grab my arm in a flash and tug me inside the darkened room. With the little light peeking through the bathroom door, I can see the fact their coat is gone.

Head to toe, their body is covered in the same black feathers as their cowl. Their feet and toes are the only slightly unnatural thing about them, with clawed talons instead of nails. They grab my face, turning it from one side to the other.

"I'm sorry. I thought I had time to get in here before it was released."

"Huh?" Staring up at them, my lips part as their thumb skates across my mouth.

"My pollination is beginning. The powder." Charlie steps closer, backing me up until I hit the door. Bending closer, they peer at me. "You're human. Why are you reacting if you're human?"

The heat in my body makes sense now. What began as a slow burn now feels uncomfortably humid. I tug at my clothes again, pressing my thighs together as I stare up at them, truly baffled. Opening my mouth, I suck in a startled breath as they cover it immediately with one of their palms.

"Stop inhaling. You'll want to fuck me if you ingest any more."

My eyes widen. *Too late.*

Charlie sighs, hanging their head. "You already want to, don't you, Winifred?" Pulling their hand away slowly, they pinch my chin with two fingers, frowning. "You look like an adult. Are you?"

"Y-Yes?"

They huff, leaning closer before their wings snap out behind them. A spray of shimmering pink powder puffs off them, the entirety of their inner membrane so clear I could read a book through it, save for the edges that are a mix of black and crimson red. As the powder settles over us both, I sneeze softly, rubbing my nose as I fidget under their gaze, feeling my nipples tighten.

"I do-do-do —" I stop myself, pressing my lips together again as I try to clear my throat.

Charlie watches me for a moment, their eyes focused on only my face. It's... unnerving, but calming.

With a swallow, I try again. "I do w-want to f-f-fu —" They wait, and I manage to get it out. "Fuck you."

Their lips twitch in a smile. "Was that an insult, or a request?"

Huffing, I scowl slightly. "Request." Sometimes single words are easier to get out, and Charlie leans back with a little laugh that makes their wings shake.

"Well, Winifred." They touch my face, gently pushing a loose strand of hair behind my ear. "You don't *seem* lost to the pollen, and that was a fairly lucid demand, all things considered. I'll let you fuck me on one condition."

The doorknob digs into my back as I force myself to

measure my breathing, waiting for them to finish their demand.

Charlie moves closer, their hand slipping down to encircle my throat. They don't apply pressure, but as I swallow, I feel their fingers stroke my skin.

"You can fuck me, but I'd like to fuck you too. It's only fair."

Standing on my toes, I jerk forward, pressing my lips against theirs with a nod. Their hand falls away, their tall body swaying as I nearly climb them like a tree. They smell... indescribably good. With my lips on theirs, I just feel heat and dizziness as their hands wrap around my thighs and lift me up and up until I can bend down to kiss them from a better angle. Instead of laying me on the bed, they sit on the edge of the mattress, pulling me into their lap to straddle them as one of their hands finds mine, guiding me to stroke up and down the soft feathers on their chest.

"Have you ever fucked a moth, Winifred?"

I shake my head as I kiss across their jaw, nudging their cheek with my nose as I breathe in the pollen again, grinding against their leg.

"My wings produce a pheromone-laced pollen every few years, meant to entice potential mates. I normally find a place to stay until the pollination season is over, but I guess my timing was off this year." They let out a little groan when I bite at their ear, reaching up to stroke the base of their antennae. The fluff in my hands wiggles as they cut off with a little gasp and I feel wetness against my belly.

Pulling back, I look down in awe as more shimmering slick secretes from their lower abdomen and the apex just above their thighs. The feathers there rustle, and then a little slit appears, pulsating softly. With one glance up at their face, I move my hand from their chest lower, stroking the edges of the slit gently.

Charlie shudders underneath me, whimpering. "If I cared to, I'd reproduce during this time, but I don't care to. I normally just fuck myself stupid until it ends."

"I c-can help with that." I flash them a little smile, feeling my fingertips slide over their slit. Up and down motions make their shoulders shake, and I tilt my head as I survey them before slowly pushing them down to the bed. They collapse with a little sigh, wings spread wide underneath them as I kiss over their feathered chest, then move lower until I reach the slit. It almost resembles a vagina, puffy and wet with arousal, so I glide my tongue over it experimentally.

They jolt under me, grabbing my upper arms with a loud moan. "Wicked little human."

Grinning, I do it again, treating them how I'd fuck myself. As I lick and stroke them, the slit grows wider and wetter, until it opens partially. Sucking a finger into my mouth, I hum at the taste, brightly floral like honeysuckle before I tease it against their entrance.

Charlie curses, writhing against the bed as their legs twitch under me. Nudging the slit open, I rub curiously against the interior, until my finger bumps a little ridge near the top that has them blabbering nonsense. With renewed focus, I dive back down, using a finger to stimulate the ridge as my tongue glides up and down the outside, only occasionally sliding in. Their arousal is addicting, and I rub my thighs together as I eat them out with a moan of my own, rubbing against their thigh.

They reach down, one hand on my hip to help me grind as I bury myself against them, barely breathing as I focus on rubbing and flicking the ridge inside them.

Charlie jolts once, their back arching as they hold onto me, gasping my name before arousal floods my mouth. It drips down my chin, like the juices of a fresh peach, soaking my front as I pull back, my finger still moving inside them. Their slit widens with each release, fluid squirting out of them once, twice, then finally, a third time before they drop back to the bed with a low moan.

Then their stimuli slide free.

I watch in awe as three tendrils emerge from their slit, twisting together and writhing through the mess they left on their own abdomen. They reach for me, and I offer my hand experimentally, feeling the tentacle-like appendages wrap around my fingers, squeezing gently before tugging me closer to them.

Charlie sits up from the bed, staring down at me with hooded eyes. “My turn.”

I gasp as they wrap their arms around me, pulling me up their chest until they can reach my lips. The kiss is filthy, all tongue as Charlie rolls me onto my back on the bed. Leaning over me, the height difference is even more apparent. They stare down at me as they tug up my soaked sweater and throw it to the side. Their hands hesitate on my jeans, and I lift my hips, licking my lips as I say, “Take t-them off.”

They smile, ridding me of my pants, then my underwear and bra, leaving me just in my socks as they lean down and kiss across my chest. It’s mostly flat in this position, but that doesn’t seem to bother them as they suckle at each nipple, the soft feathers around their throat making me fidget against the bed as I feel the tendrils map my thighs, slick and searching. Charlie pulls away, breathing hard as they open my thighs wide, kneeling above me. The tendrils twist together, forming a writhing length that dips down on its own accord to slide across my clit.

With a whimper, I roll my hips toward them, staring as their wings flare out again. A fresh layer of pollen dusts over us, leaving me shaking with pleasure as the tendrils search lower and lower until their combined head teases at my entrance. With a little thrust, they seat the tendrils inside of me just before all three unfurl from each other, stretching wide. The sensation is so fucking different from anything else I've ever felt — especially when all three move independently of each other to stroke my inner walls until one finds my g-spot.

I come off the bed with a gasp, clawing at Charlie's forearms as they pant with a little grin. "You drove me crazy. Let me return the favor, Winifred."

The tendril on my g-spot drills into it with precision as the other two thrust in and out. The sound is lewd when I clench around them, one hand dropping to the bed as the pleasure overtakes my senses. Charlie bends, moving their hips faster to help the tendrils as they fuck me. One of them slips free and instead of rejoining the others, it teases against my ass, circling the tight hole until it wiggles inside.

"Y-Yes!" I cry out, my body shaking at the overstimulation. Just as my eyes shut, I see Charlie's wings shake. Burning desire ignites inside me as I scream, coming around them until I'm nothing but a shaking, sweating mess on the bed. Charlie keeps thrusting, the tendril stroking my g-spot over and over again until I dig my nails into their forearm, shaking my head. "I can't, C-Charlie."

They groan, then their lips are on mine, surging forward with determination as one hand slips between us. Their fingers find my clit, and it's over. The second orgasm takes the breath from my lungs as I jolt against them, my release combining with theirs and soaking us both. I feel it drip out of me and down my thighs as they pull back with a breathless laugh. When I look between us, I see the cum mixing with the shimmering pollen on my skin, streaking up my body like glitter.

Charlie kisses my jaw, then my cheek, smiling against my skin. "Sorry, that will take forever to wash off."

"I l-like it." Running my finger through a puddle of the mixture on my stomach, I lift my hand and suck it into my mouth, the burst of floral flavor making me moan softly. "F-Fuck me again?"

They lift their head, watching me with hooded eyes before nodding. "Until the sun rises?"

Touching their cowl, I pull them closer, careful of the feathers as I kiss them with a little nod. "Yes." They take my mouth in another deep kiss, and I sink into the bed as the tendrils tease at my swollen holes again, the pollen making my head spin with heady desire.

I don't speak another word until morning.

STRAIGHT TO VOICEMAIL

IT WAS JUST BEFORE FIVE.

Normally, Siobhan worked until six. It depended on the day, quite frankly, and was highly likely she'd do anything to finish *before* six on lighter call days. But a siren's job was very rarely completed before the end of business hours.

I, of course, liked to bother her before she was done.

With one last glance at our simmering dinner on the stove, I ease the door to her office open, smiling as I watch her twist back and forth in her office chair. Her full tawny brown wings flare over the sides, relaxed and dragging the ground. I've only seen her in her aquatic form a few times — really just last year when we *finally* went on a vacation together to the beach.

Looking up from her desktop screen, Siobhan pushes her glasses up her nose with a tiny smile, her sharp teeth flashing in the dim light. "Hello, baby, I'm just waiting for my last call."

I pad into the room, wrapping my arms around my girlfriend from behind with a tiny smile, peppering kisses across her bronze jaw as I hum. She's like a plant, always in the sun when she's not trapped behind a screen. "I figured. Dinner will be done soon. Who are you waiting for this time?"

She runs her hands over my forearms, tilting her head and pursing her lips. With a little laugh, I bend down and kiss her gently, cupping her face with a hand.

"Just a consultation for some business." Waving a hand, she sighs against my lips before pulling me around her and toward her lap. Cupping my hips, she pulls me partially on top of her, shaking her head. "They want to know their life's desire and destiny." Rolling her eyes, Siobhan glances at her screen again. "They have twenty-three minutes before their call window is over. I'm *not* picking up late again."

I kiss all over her jaw, glancing down at her casual clothes. She gets to work all day in pajamas while I'm running back and forth to the magic shop with potions and small spell work bundles that sell like hotcakes. I wouldn't trade it for the world though. It's very fulfilling to be a witch who is actually making my own living without being hired by another being as their private spell-caster.

My eyes dip to her tiny shorts riding up the skin of her thighs. When I glance back up at her, Siobhan's cheeks are slightly darker. "Dani..."

"It's Daniela," I purr, kissing down her throat and pulling her cardigan to the side so I can run my tongue over the soft skin at the top of her collarbones. "Or mommy, whichever you prefer this evening."

She lets out a little whine, wiggling in her chair. "What if they call?"

"I guess you should hold off on audibly moaning into the phone." With a smirk, I slip off her lap, kneeling partially under her desk as I use her chair to pull her closer to me. Palming her thighs, I pull them wider, watching her skin shimmer. There's something about sirens that makes their forms change depending on the partner they've chosen — I don't mind, I like seeing her splayed out stark naked in our bed while every muscle in her body and her wings twitch with pleasure.

Her skin ripples, the hidden scales under her flesh responding as I urge her hips up. Siobhan lets out a plaintive sound. "Please, baby."

"Please, what?" Hooking my fingers under her shorts, I tug them off, clicking my tongue as I do. "You're bare *again*, Siobhan? You've been sitting in this chair all day with your pussy wet, hoping I'd come in here and have my dessert before dinner?"

Her curly hair topples to one side as she hiccups and nods. "I like it when you do."

"Yeah?" Her thighs feel like silk under my fingertips as I spread her wider, kissing across her skin before I reach the apex of her thighs and breathe in the smell of her arousal from the source. The caramel brown hair on her mound matches the color on her head as I kiss the area right above her clit. "You like it when your witch is on her knees, baby?"

She sighs, sliding a hand into my hair. When she relaxes back into the chair, her legs splay wider. One lifts, thrown over the arm of the office chair as I pull her lips apart and glide my tongue from ass to clit once, humming at the taste. I don't know what fucking god I pleased in a past life to be blessed with her in this one, but I'm never taking it for granted.

Siobhan grunts, rolling herself forward a bit as I nudge at her clit with my tongue, circling and flicking it as her other hand reaches down to grasp at my shoulder. Her fingers massage my trap muscles as I close my eyes, working around her clit with the flat of my tongue as I feel the arousal begin to gather against my chin. She makes the sweetest little sounds as I pull back and lick my lips, dragging a finger through her wetness before thrusting it carefully into her.

Jerking against the chair, her mouth drops open, her eyes going dark. The pupils expand, overtaking the normal blue of her irises as her siren side bleeds out. With parted lips, Siobhan's next whimper turns into a lilting wail, almost musical as I crook my finger, rubbing her inner walls with slow strokes.

"Poor little siren." I add a second finger, watching her wings twitch as her chest heaves. "So wet and ready to be fucked. Tell me, what's my greatest desire right now?"

Her eyelids flutter as she gasps out, "You want to bend me over my desk."

Grinning to myself, I nudge her g-spot with two fingers, stroking it gently as she trembles. "Yes, I do, baby. Are you getting flashes of that right now?"

Her head jerks as she babbles, lost to the vision, "Yes. I see you with the big one. The one that barely fits and you've got me by the hair and you're — *oh.*" Her wet pussy clenches around my fingers as I feel the ripple expand through her muscles. Sliding my fingers free, I suck them into my mouth, laughing as she lets out a loud gasp.

"Take your top off. Now."

She complies in an instant, sitting up straight in the chair and whipping off her cardigan and the loose shirt she has on. With her hands in her lap, she blinks down at me, biting her lower lip and whispering, "How do you want me?"

Kneeling on the floor, my eyes dart up to the desk. "How long do they have to call?"

Siobhan's eyes widen as she looks back at the clock. "Seventeen minutes."

I get back to my feet, brushing off the knees of my leggings. "Good, sit there naked until I get back. Don't touch yourself."

Her mouth pops open as I stride out of the room. I give her the grace of waiting until I'm back in the living room before I quietly cackle to myself and make a beeline for our bedroom.

Her siren senses *were* right, I've wanted her bent over her desk for days. As my hand wraps around the harness I left on the bed, I rid myself of all of my clothes save for my lace bra and underwear, fidgeting a little at how the gusset is already sticking to my damp cunt.

Refusing to focus on it, I instead slide the harness on, reaching for the dildo she saw in her vision. It's almost as huge as my forearm, but *god* it looks so fucking good when she's struggling to take it. I grab a small bottle of lube too, sweeping my hair up into a high ponytail before I stride back to her office.

She's still perched on her seat, her shoulders moving just slightly faster than normal with each breath she takes. The bottle cap of the lube snaps as I open it, making her jolt and her wings shake as I watch her struggle not to turn around.

"Stand up and bend over your desk, Siobhan."

She rushes to comply, pushing the office chair out of the way for me without looking behind herself. Her wings drag on the ground as she bends over, putting her ass in the air as her head rests on her arms. Visible wetness slicks between her thighs as I pump my hand over the strap, preparing it for her.

Saying a quiet spell under my breath to activate the dildo, I stride toward her, running my hand between her thighs to smear the lube and her arousal.

"You want me, little siren?"

"Yes, mommy." Siobhan wiggles, breathless and barely audible. "Gods, fuck me, Dani."

My hand pulls away from her just to return to her pussy with a hard smack. She yelps, then pushes her ass into me, her back arching. "Do whatever you want to me."

The words are music to my ears as I reach forward and wrap her hair around my fist twice. Siobhan lets out a breath, which turns into a lulling whine as I use my other hand to guide the tip of the dildo against her entrance. Teasing her with a slow roll of my hips, my eyes practically cross as the full effects of the spell hit me in my lower stomach. I spent *hours* doing work on this specific dildo so I could feel like *I* was actually the one entering her, fucking her, making her come all over me, and the sparks go straight to my clit as she whines and writhes as I pulse my hips. Her cunt stretches over the girth as Siobhan lets out little gasped moans, rising higher on her toes.

"Oh *fuck*, it's too big, it's too much, it's —" She cuts herself off with a cry that makes a shiver crawl up my spine as I slip in further. The next words out of her mouth are laced with her siren's call. "Don't you *fucking* dare stop."

Grinning, I jerk her head back by her hair and slam deeper. She yelps, but presses against me, the backs of her thighs and ass almost meeting my thrusts. Siobhan's head tilts, her neck arching as I work in further, pushing and pushing until we're flush against each other and she's panting. It's only then that I move my hand from her hip and wrap it around her throat, lifting her so her back and wings are against my chest.

She writhes like a cat in heat, pressing against the coarseness of my lace bra as I fuck her, barely pulling my hips back before I slam up into her. Her cries go from broken to melodic, filling the air with a heady sound as her hands slam onto the desk to keep herself upright.

I slip two fingers into her mouth, hissing as I bottom out again, my clit twitching with the magic. "Careful, you're getting a call, siren."

Spittle leaks past my fingers as she makes a muffled sound, her head moving slightly to stare at her desktop as it lights up with a call from her client — at the last possible minute they can.

I feel her pussy tighten, fluttering as I whisper, "Are you answering it? Or are you letting it go to voicemail so your mommy can finish fucking you properly like the little office slut you are?"

Siobhan shakes for a moment, then she moves a hand to reach for the mouse, sending the call to voicemail.

"Good choice." I pull out of her and then pound back in like a woman possessed. Her upper body drops to the desktop as her wings flare out under me. Feathers rustle as I hold onto her hips and pump into her hard and fast. Her cries echo off the walls, surely loud enough for any of our supernaturally gifted neighbors to hear as she shrieks and pushes back against me.

"Please! Please make me come, mommy!"

Pulling my hand back, I slap her on the side of her ass, feeling her muscles tighten as sweat beads on my brow. I puff out a breath and hold onto her hips, focusing on driving into her as her toes scramble for purchase on the wooden floor. Pushing her ass back against me, Siobhan buries her face in the desktop, crying out against the wood as she gasps, "Yes, *yes*, there, *please*."

"Here?" I angle my hips down slightly, letting the strap drill into her as I drop a hand from her hip to under us. Her clit is hard as a rock when I find it, flicking it once. "You ready to come, baby?"

She cries out, gasping as I pinch her clit, then shudders under me, falling apart with a mournful wail that makes every piece of glass in the apartment ripple with the sound. Laughing, I keep moving into her, feeling myself near my own orgasm as her cunt milks the dildo for all it's worth. With two more thrusts, I moan, clinging to her as pleasure washes over me, making me come so hard I can't think for a moment as I soak my underwear.

Under me, Siobhan moans, rolling her neck back and forth. "That was just as good as I hoped."

Licking my lips, I throw my head back, groaning. "I really hope I didn't let dinner burn."

She giggles, wiggling herself back until she presses against me. The softness of her wings stroke against my thighs. "They're going to be so pissed I sent them straight to voicemail."

With a self-assured grin, I pull out of her, unlocking the harnèss only to let it drop to the floor in a mess. "Too damn bad. You had other plans."

Siobhan sighs, getting up to stand on shaking legs before she turns to look at me. Her eyes droop, hooded as she takes me in, licking her lips slowly. As she smiles, her voice comes out slightly husky. "Did you soak those expensive underwear for me, Dani? I bet I could tell you every last desire you have."

Goosebumps rise on my skin as I let her devour me with her eyes. "They're ruined. You better get on your knees and clean it up."

She slips to the floor with grace, her wings fluttering as she grabs my thighs and pulls me forward until my cunt is lined up with her mouth. Siobhan stares up at me, breathing hard. "Yes, mommy."

STRAWBERRY RED

God, if my coworkers could see me now, they'd never call me boring again.

I slide my fingers up and down the glass stem of the strawberry daiquiri in my hands. The club's music rolls over me, a soft din that fills the open hall and compliments the diffused green lights illuminating the floor.

Behind the bar, I watch the djinn bartender teleport back and forth, moving faster than anyone else could as they puff in and out of existence in front of customers. They conjure drinks out of thin air, putting on a show for the various other patrons that litter the other bar stools making a circle around the bar. I went to a Vegas magic show with djinn performers a couple years ago and they'd done the same to the audience — appearing at random intervals to twirl and spin before disappearing in a cloud of smoke.

It's a bit unnecessary to make the bartender turn tricks while pouring glasses of wine, but that seems to be the draw of an interspecies sex club — other than the sex, of course.

Pulling my glass closer, I take another small sip, glancing

around. There's some kind of cat shifter down the bar, half shifted with her tail out as she chats with a tall, willowy looking man with shadows lingering around his form. The various bar top tables that scatter the floor have the occasional couple talking over glasses.

A small *puff* is the only alert I get before the djinn appears in front of me, flashing me a small smile. "Need anything, human?"

I let out a laugh, glancing at their smooth green skin and the creases around their eyes. They're attractive with a broad crooked nose and angled eyebrows, but the thought of flirting back makes my stomach churn, swirling the alcohol in it into a whirlpool.

"No, thank you." I take another sip for something to do, chewing on my lower lip while gazing at the open room.

"You know." The bartender leans against the back of the bar, eyeing me for a second. "We do tours on these open nights. I can flag someone down to walk you around."

My mouth flounders open and shut, processing the words. It is the *logical* step to coming to an open night of the club, but the idea of wandering around the large building, likely one of the only humans in the place, makes anxiety rise in my blood.

I'd picked this club for a reason — a little out of the way, not likely to be frequented by my coworkers, or anyone else I know day-to-day — and the club's online calendar listed some of their past voyeur hall demonstrations.

Running my tongue over my lips, I glance again at the door to the hall, marked by a small sign that has the times for tonight's demonstration.

"You can go in." The bartender is closer when I look back at them. "Take your drink, go watch the shibari demo and enjoy yourself. I promise no one will bite." They pause, then grin. "Unless you're into that, of course." They wink at me before puffing away in a wisp of smoke, appearing in front of the cat shifter and her date.

My grip on the glass is so tight, I'm briefly afraid I'll shatter it as I slide off my barstool. Sucking in a breath, I walk across the floor, side-stepping a pair of vampires standing at a bar table and chatting over wine glasses full of blood. As I near the door, my hair ruffles around my shoulders in a flash of wind. I blink once and jolt at the sight of the vampires in front of me. Both of the women give me a fanged smile as one holds the door open.

Mumbling a thank you, I step into the intimate room behind them.

It's half the size of the main hall, with matching black walls and flooring. At the center of the room a slightly raised platform stands, leaving patrons space to gather around in clusters. Some of the viewers speak to each other in soft tones, while others watch the display happening on stage.

A short and thin-limbed volunteer hangs, bound in a tangle of ropes, with a blissed-out expression. It's a firm juxtaposition to the demonstrator circling him purposefully.

"You want to make sure your knots are secure." The demonstrator's husky and low voice rolls over the crowd. I keep near the back, biting my tongue at the way he touches the volunteer's body, tightening the joining ropes and lifting them with no effort. "The last thing you want to do is hurt your submissive, especially if they're gagged and can't use their safe word. Which is why we also have safety measures and hand signals."

The man circles the stage to show the other side of the crowd the double knot against the volunteer's back. My eyes focus on his thick hands as they move deftly over the rope, tugging on various sides to demonstrate how each one moves the volunteer in different directions.

"It comes down to trust." The demonstrator flashes the crowd a smile with bright white teeth and slightly long canines. A chunk of blond hair falls out of the knot of a bun at the top of his head. "Everything you want to experiment with needs to be built on a foundation of trust."

My eyes run over him as I take a tiny sip of my drink. His broad shoulders make his shirt strain across the muscles in his upper body. As he unties the volunteer slowly, he walks the crowd through the proper ways to release them. His hands rub and squeeze over the other man's body, soothing where the ropes were pressed into the volunteer's skin. Offering the volunteer a hand, he lets him stand fully, supporting him now that he's no longer suspended mid-air and at the demonstrator's mercy.

"You did a great job." The demonstrator smiles, nodding at everyone. "Didn't he? I think our volunteer deserves a round of applause."

A scatter of applause breaks out, polite and encouraging as the demonstrator helps the volunteer off the platform. I watch as he slides a hand over the man's shoulder at the last second, squeezing it and dipping to say something soft. The volunteer gives him a pleased smile in return.

Sticking back against the wall, I linger as the demonstrator begins to rewind the ropes, using his arms as anchor points. He moves fluidly, up and down, until the two ropes are in manageable twists, coiled around one another. When he finishes, he picks up a water bottle from the side of the platform, draining it. His throat moves, bobbing with the action and I get an obscene flash of heat in my stomach at the sight of a few droplets running down his chin.

Blinking, I take a side-step back, shaking my head to clear it. The room is mostly empty, the final few patrons leaving through the door back to the main hall. Turning toward it, I clear my throat, trying to swallow past a lump of nerves from being left alone. I should have stayed at the bar, finished my drink, and then gone home—

"First time?"

I jolt at the sound of the deep voice just behind me. The demonstrator walks slowly, like he's afraid to spook me as he carries the ropes to a chest tucked against the wall that I hadn't noticed. Now that he's bent over it, I can see it's full of supplies, including different types of rope and a few spare bottles of water.

Up close, he's at least a foot and a half taller than me, and I'm already pushing six feet. His skin glows almost golden in the dim light as he rises up, closing the trunk just to give me a smile.

"It's okay, not a lot of people know what they're doing when they walk in here for the first time." His eyes take me in, pausing at my drink. "We don't get a lot of humans, either."

I balk at him, hearing nothing but the heartbeat racing in my ears and the bass of the music in the other room. "I—how did you know?"

He motions at the drink. "I could smell the rum and strawberry syrup all the way up there." His head nods at the empty platform and my heart flips when he gives me a teasing look. "And *you*."

Fidgeting with my glass, I look down at myself, too self-aware of the little green dress I threw on after work, when I'd made the split-second decision to show up tonight. It does scream *human*, nowhere near as sleek as the other outfits I've seen tonight. I bought it from a sale rack because the color compliments the red in my hair.

His voice is softer when he speaks again. "What's your name?"

Raising my eyes, I chew on the inside of my cheek. "Ines."

His gaze burns as he watches me, at a respectful distance, but clearly curious to step closer.

"I'm Ellis." He holds out a hand that I eye before taking. His palm engulfs mine, warm and lightly calloused. The same smile from the stage lights up Ellis's features. "Has anyone shown you around the club?"

"Oh." My hand tingles as his hand brushes my skin before pulling away. "No, not yet."

"Well, we have open nights for a reason." Ellis winks, before he slips his hands into his pockets. "Let me give you a tour, Ines. It'll be worth it, especially if you're considering a membership here."

I don't know what it is about him that makes me flounder so much, but I can only nod when he steps closer. He uses a hand, just hovering around my hip, to guide us both toward the main room. Over my head, Ellis tugs the door open again to let us both back into the main club area, his voice husky at my back.

"I'm sure you've seen this area; we have the main stage which we use a few times a month for shows. My favorite are the burlesque events." His head dips, mouth close to my ear. "And you've seen the bar, which I think is a personal highlight for me."

My cheeks heat as I toy with my glass, turning my head to look up at him. I catch his eyes sparkling in the dim light, and he's shameless as he looks down at me, taking me in again. A tiny thrill coasts up my spine as his hand ghosting over my hip nears just enough to touch. Ellis navigates us past the bar-top tables and to a pair of seats around the circular bar itself.

I leave my glass on the bar as I back onto a seat.

"There's a private entrance at the front. We wanted separation from visitors and actual club members. It helps make everyone comfortable." Ellis's tone is casual, but his eyes never leave me. “We have this hall, the demonstration hall, and then the voyeur hall.”

Sucking on my bottom lip, I tilt my head to follow his gaze to a door with a bulky security guard stationed next to it. If I didn’t know we were in a sex club, he’d look bored to anyone else. I guess if you’ve seen one threesome, you’ve seen them all.

“Would you like to see the voyeur hall, Ines?”

The way he whispers my name makes my stomach flip as I glance back at him. Ellis inclines his head toward me, waiting for my approval.

With a slight nod, I smooth my hands over my thighs. “Maybe just a peek.”

The growl that reverberates through his chest makes me blush. He shifts closer for a heartbeat, hesitating before his hand slides across my back and presses against my dress. His body radiates heat as he moves me off my stool and escorts me to the door. The security barely glances at him before allowing us both to walk through.

I don’t know what I expected, but a dark and narrow hallway isn’t it. There are two clear sides of pathways, lit by little lights running along the flooring. The red bulbs illuminate my heels as I approach the first window open to a room.

All the air leaves my lungs as I just stand and *watch*.

A gorgon woman splays out on her stomach across a chaise, her ass in the air as her torso brushes the leather. Behind her, a man looms, hips pumping hard and quick as his hands map her body, avoiding the tangle of snakes making up her hair. The snakes don’t look irritated, but they are writhing in pleasure as she throws her head back, her lips parting as her partner fucks her.

A perverse coil of pleasure unfurls in me, unable to bear looking away. The sight is enrapturing as the man’s nails elongate into claws, making red scratches on the woman’s skin as he drags them over her. She arches, clinging to the leather underneath her as her body is marked by him.

"We have healers on our staff in case anything gets out of hand." Ellis's voice in my ear makes goosebumps rise on my arms. He's so close behind me that the musky scent of him — sweat and something spiced — invades my senses. We both stare into the room as his hand touches my back again. "But we welcome humans just as much as we welcome anyone else. This place is about releasing your inhibitions, not fearing your own desire."

My tongue wets my lips as I nod, unsure if I can speak with the way his voice lights up my body.

Moving down the path, I follow the flow of patrons to the next window. Behind this one a minotaur stands, hands tangled in the hair of a woman on her knees in front of him. Her throat bulges with every rock of his hips as his thick cock forces its way between her lips. She chokes on it, spit and cum dripping past as her eyes stay locked on his, completely determined.

Heat lances through me as the minotaur makes her head bob, before pulling her off of him. An unspoken, silent moment passes between the pair as she openly pants before dropping lower and running her tongue down his length to his balls.

Ellis makes a strangled noise in his throat behind me. I turn just as he slips past, drawn to the next display. Dragging myself away from the sight of the minotaur's thick cock bobbing against the woman's face, I slow to a stop next to Ellis.

This room only contains a single naga. His coiled snake half encompasses easily half the floor space as his body leans on what can only be described as a throne. The chair rocks back precariously on two legs every time the naga pumps both his weeping cocks, each hand busy matching the same pace and rhythm. His head rolls against the throne, lost and unconcerned with those watching as he gets himself off.

When I look up at the side of Ellis's face, his eyes are narrowed, singularly focused. Sliding my hand over his arm, I can't help the spike of desire as his throat bobs, lips parting, and eyes darting briefly from the window to me. Slipping past him, I walk around the end of the hall and cross over to the other side of display windows, letting him have a moment to enjoy the naga alone.

A werewolf, half-shifted, bends a man over in one room. Two witches tangle together in another. A full orgy is happening in a third window. I can't stop to stare at any of them, my throat feeling unnaturally tight and my dress suddenly feeling extremely warm. Cool air hits my skin as I leave the hall, pressing a hand to the side of my neck while I try to fight the violent flushing overtaking my entire body.

Do I want to be on display like those people? Or could I lose myself in watching for hours as they all indulge in every hedonistic desire they want for just tonight?

Ellis appears after another heartbeat. His chuckle is light, but knowing as he pulls me back to the bar where the djinn notices us immediately. They slide over a cool water bottle with a wink before disappearing again.

Focusing on unscrewing the lid, I breathe in and out as Ellis talks softly about some of the club's other amenities. As he angles closer, not quite sitting on the stool next to me, but instead taking up the space between my stool and the other, my legs part, allowing him to be boxed in between them and the bar.

He watches me as I finally take a drink, a smile on his face. "We hold demonstrations at least three times a week." Running a thumb over his lower lip, Ellis looks up at the ceiling in thought. "I can't speak to all our clientele, but a lot of the humans that visit or that have a membership come with inter-species partners." His eyes dart back to me. "Not all, but many. Can I ask how you found us?"

My grip tightens on the water bottle. "Well..."

"You don't have to answer. I'm just curious."

Shaking my head to clear my muddled thoughts, I inhale sharply. "I found you online, actually. I was..." I trail off, staring down the bar to confirm the djinn is busy with others, leaving the space between us just for my admission. It won't help if there's others with enhanced hearing, but it's easier to speak when I look back at Ellis and take in his open expression. "I was searching for someone specific."

One of his eyebrows rises.

"Wait, oh god." I lean away from him, my mouth popping open. "Not like that!" Unbidden images of species fetishists flash through my mind — all the sick and twisted things probably going through *his* too. Quickly, I hold out a hand. "I saw that *you* had a demonstration on impact play last week, but it was for members only. The only demonstration you were hosting tonight was bondage."

Ellis's face morphs from genuine confusion to mirth as he laughs, bracing a hand on the bar. It brings him closer to me, sending my stomach fluttering again as he tilts his head. "So you waited until you knew I'd be here to visit."

My cheeks heat as I nod, fidgeting with the water bottle. The plastic crinkles as his eyes pinch at the edges. "I — well —" My nerves scatter into the wind. This was a *bad* idea and —

His hand moves from the bar to brush over my arm. Jolting, I look back at him as his smile turns easy. "We don't have to talk about this if it makes you uncomfortable, but you clearly came here tonight for a reason." His fingers graze over the hair of my forearm, sending it prickling. "I'd like to help, even if it's just pointing you in the right direction or helping you find the membership option that would fit." Ellis shifts closer, tilting his head down. The action causes a few pieces of blond hair to slip free from his bun, framing his features. "Or I could help you find someone you'd feel comfortable exploring your desires with."

I force myself to swallow, my mouth feeling bone dry. His shoulders angle toward me, helping to create the illusion it's just the two of us in the room. As his fingers dance over my skin, I wet my lips again, my mind peacefully quiet as his touch grounds me.

"I want to stop thinking." My voice is barely above a whisper. "I want someone who will bend me over and take control. I'm so *tired* of being the one in control."

His touch stutters for the briefest of moments before resuming as I tilt my head, completely caught in his gaze.

"I'm always the person who has to put the fires out. I'm always the one rushing to finish a task no one else completed. I'm always the back-up. I'm the one people call because, '*Ines can do that tonight. She has time.*' I saw the impact play demonstration on the calendar and all I could think was that I wanted *that*. I want to *know* what it feels like to be at someone's mercy, but also trust them implicitly to hurt me only in the ways I want, to *use* me but with my own limits in mind. Isn't that what kinks are for? Should I not explore what I want and find what feels good to me instead of feeling constantly beholden to everyone else?"

The words hang in the air before I make myself shift away from him, my chest tight. "I'm sorry. That was — I should go."

Ellis moves in a flash. His hand flattens on my arm. It's not invasive — and if I slid off the stool I could leave — but it would bring me chest to chest with him. Something crackles in the air between us as he licks his lips.

"I can let you go." My body cools at his words, before the

temperature feels like it's been turned to a thousand degrees in an instant. "Or I can show you the private rooms upstairs where we can finish this conversation like the adults we are."

He pulls away to perch on the stool opposite me.

Two nights ago, I turned my laptop on and searched everything I could think of — finally at my wit's end. I wanted to *learn*, but also let go. I'm so tired of mainlining coffee and going on runs at dawn to circumvent myself from losing my shit on every single person in the office.

I leave the water bottle on the bar as we survey each other.

"I'd like to see a private room." The words roll off my tongue before I add at the last second, "Please?"

A smile crawls across his face as his hand smooths over my arm and picks up my hand. Ellis guides me off the barstool before we make our way to a small spiral staircase in the corner that leads to the second floor. A security guard at the top actually stops Ellis to speak quietly, and I peer around them to see a couch and table. To a side is a desk where a horned woman sits behind a computer, her forked tail flicking in the air behind her to the beat of the music downstairs.

Ellis leads me past security and the woman looks up, brightening at the sight of us. "Oh!"

"Just a room, Mars." Ellis smiles coyly. "Not twenty questions."

Her eyes dart to me, then back to Ellis as her lips purse in a little pleased smile. "Of course, you big stupid lion." After typing rapidly, she scans a keycard and then holds it out to me with a flourish. "Here you go, my dear. Enjoy yourself!"

Taking the card from her red fingers, I feel myself blush as Ellis walks me to a closed door. The hallway behind it is even darker than the voyeur hall, with a branching *t* of corridors that are lined with doors instead of windows. To the right, Ellis guides me to the furthest room and I press the card against the lock, breathing out as I feel him at my back.

The sensor switches from red to green and I open the door to a room very similar to the decor downstairs. The black tile floor has a rug near a four-poster bed on the far wall. To the left is a small kitchenette with a sink, mini fridge, and bar cart laden with bottles all clustered together. Spinning in a circle, I take in the cabinet opposite of the kitchenette, and finally, two chairs with a small table between them forming a sitting area.

The noise from the club dampens to nothing as Ellis shuts the door with a click.

He walks past me to fiddle with the light coming from two lamps, dimming the brightness to a warm yellow glow that permeates the room. Then he scans the bar cart before stooping to pluck a water bottle from the mini fridge. He places it on the counter for a moment before focusing on rolling up the sleeves of his shirt, exposing a myriad of tattoos crawling up his golden skin.

"She called you a lion," I blurt, distracted by the sight of the corded muscles on his arms. He opens the water as I fidget with the keycard between two fingers.

Ellis looks up, taking a drink. "She did. I am one. I never know if humans want to know immediately, or if you all like the thrill of puzzling out what I am by yourselves."

A small laugh escapes. "It's not very polite to speculate on someone else's species. I've just never met a lion. At least... I don't think I have." The plastic grows warm between my fingers. "My boss is a dragon."

Ellis's smile makes my toes curl. "An actual one, or just an asshole?"

"A little of both, maybe?"

His rolling laughter fills the room, deep and warm. My shoulders relax at the sound. Ellis leans against the counter, humming. "There's a lot of species that fall under the category of lions. There's feline shifters, of course, but also Sphinx, Komainu, and Nemean Lions descended from the Greeks. There's also snow lions from Tibet." He ticks off a finger for each one, then flashes me all his teeth. "Then you have me."

Raising an eyebrow at him, I fight back a smile. "Dare I ask?"

He flexes his shoulders, glancing off to the side before he reaches behind himself and tugs his shirt off in one smooth motion, exposing his tattooed chest. I only see a glimpse of it before huge, golden feathered wings spring from nowhere on his back. The shift is so fast, it blows me away as he shakes out his hair from his bun. The illusion of it falling around his shoulders forms a mane — still human-like, but not entirely as he taps a singular shifted claw on the counter.

"A winged lion, descended from Italian royals." He looks at me, his eyelids lowering as he takes me in. "We're the best of them all. I don't full-shift on the first date, but if you ask nicely, I'll show you my tail later."

A giggle bubbles up as I stare at him, reconciling in my mind that he can be a lion whenever he wants. Not only that — but one that can *fly*.

His eyes sparkle with delight at the sound of my laughter, then his wings disappear. Ellis tugs his shirt back on, nodding at the chairs. "Do you want to sit and talk, Ines?"

I bite my tongue, nodding before I leave the keycard on the table between the pair of seats. Ellis steps over, taking the chair farthest from the door. The sheer size of him near me again makes my heart skitter in my chest as I settle carefully on the edge of the seat cushion.

"What do you know about impact play?" He dives in immediately, putting his water on the table between us. "Do you have any prior experience with it?"

Fisting my hands in my lap, I make myself meet his eyes. "I had an ex that I brought it up to. I asked if he would ever consider incorporating it — because I liked the idea of it — not punching or slapping, but the feeling of someone... jarring me? He couldn't even comprehend it, so it was off the table pretty fast." I force a smile, the pang of remembering the guy's face smarting in my chest. He'd made me feel pretty shitty about it at the end of the day.

"Which is fine." I try to cover the silence, watching Ellis tilt his head at me. "It was past his limits and I accepted that. We used safe words — the stoplight method — when we tried new things once in a blue moon. But it was all only what he wanted to try. This is my first time at a club, seeking out a kink."

His face gives nothing away as he listens to me ramble. Bracing his elbows on his knees, Ellis bends slightly. "How far do you want this to go tonight? Do you want it to end at a conversation, or are you open to exploration?"

Butterflies take off in my stomach. For as hot as I found him standing on the platform, wrapping the volunteer in ropes while constantly checking in, it's different than being the object of his singular focus.

"I —" Stuttering, I rub my hands against my dress. "Are you asking if I want to fuck you?"

Ellis's lips quirk, his expression melting into something dangerous. "I don't need to ask, I can smell that you want to. I'm asking if you're only looking to chat tonight, or if you want the experience of being bent over while I turn your ass red."

The idea that he can sense my arousal sends another spike of desire through me as my body heats. I squirm in the seat, my lips parting as I glance from him to the bed.

"Ines —" His soft tone draws my attention back to him. "You seem to be completely oblivious to the way you draw attention in every space you're in. If you think I was the only monster looking at you tonight, you're wrong. And trust me, I was looking. I just don't want to cross any boundaries, which is why we're having an informed conversation before this goes any further."

Swallowing thickly, I bob my head. "I want to understand but I also..." My eyes find the bed again.

"You also what, fragola?" The Italian that rolls off his tongue makes me shiver. Ellis reaches out, putting a hand on my knee as he purrs. "You're as sweet as a ripe strawberry, aren't you? The same color as your pink cheeks, your shiny hair, and your scent."

Blushing at the compliment, I feel a surge of confidence. "I want you to bend me over and turn my ass red, Ellis."

"That can be arranged." Cupping my knee with his hand, he raises an eyebrow at me. "Tell me your safe words."

"Red for full stop." I recite them on instinct. "Yellow for slow down and reassess. Green for keep going."

"Good." He licks his lips, looking over at the cabinet. "The demonstration you missed out on was about different equipment — whips, flogs, and hands. Do you have a preference?"

"Let's start with hands." I look down at his palm on my knee. "Just for the first time."

Ellis smiles, his eyes softening. "We can do that. Next time if you want to try something else, I'll have you use it on me first. It's far easier to control the impact with a hand, but the sensation changes."

I blush, shaking my head at him. Ellis just smiles at me as he slides out of his chair. "Ines." My name on his lips feels dangerous, sending a shiver of desire up my spine as my knees shake a little. He moves to kneel in front of my chair, head tilted so he can stare up at me, eyes dark.

I stare at his lips for a moment, then whisper, "I don't

know what I expected when I came here tonight, but it wasn't you."

His eyes flash gold. "I'm glad you came." Innuendo hangs in the air as we both breathe in. The tension stretches as I watch him place his hand gently back on my knee, warm and steady through the fabric of my dress. That same desire as before strikes through me at the sheer size of him compared to me. With his fingers splayed over my knee, the sensation is all-encompassing, but still restrained. To anyone else, it's an unassuming action, but to me it feels like a brand. This is what I asked for — to be the object of his touch for only tonight, and to let that wash away anything else in my mind for a few hours of peace.

His hand squeezes once. "I have one more question for you."

"Yes?"

"Will you let me make you feel good?" Ellis touches my other knee, parting his lips as my heart speeds up in my chest. "I'm going to make sure there isn't a single thought left in that pretty little head when I'm done with you."

All the air leaves my lungs with a little gasp. "Yes. *Please.* I just want to stop thinking." His hands slowly pull my knees open, my dress riding up as I whisper, "I just want to feel good."

The sight of him in front of me makes me feel both powerful and like this is a dream. He smirks, nodding once before rising to stand. Towering above me, he touches my cheek and tilts my head to meet his eyes. "From this point on, you listen to me, fragola. You don't have to call me anything but Ellis, but I want verbal answers to every question I ask. You *will* use your safe words both when I ask and if anything crosses a line, are we clear?"

My lips part, voice breathy. "Yes."

He steps away, his touch leaving my face before he eyes me in the chair. Every muscle in my body trembles for a moment as I tense, trying not to fidget, but still smoothing my hands over my skirt, unsure what his plans are for me.

"Stand up."

Pushing from the chair, I stare at his outstretched hand for a solid second before taking it. Ellis walks backwards, moving us toward the bed. The dark sheets look as soft as silk spread over the wide mattress. The four-poster style is all iron, with bars running along the top of the canopy instead of fabric.

Ellis sits on the edge of the mattress, then pats his lap. "Come here."

My heels slip a little when I step onto the rug next to the bed, but he's there, guiding me down to his lap. His hands smooth over me as my stomach meets the tops of his thighs, my body settling over him prone.

"That's it. That's a good girl." His hands move with me as I shiver at the term, and he allows me to shift until I feel a bit better about being bent over him. The cool air brushes the backs of my thighs as my dress rides up. "Look at you." Ellis growls slightly and it rumbles through his chest and into my body as I drop myself lower, stretching my arms out to touch the bed. My shoulders relax as his fingers dance up and down my back.

With his palms against the small of my back, he applies the slightest bit of pressure to force me flush against him. "Such a good girl for me. Tell me a color."

I sigh, feeling like a cat settling into its owner's lap. "Green." Smiling, I let my head fall, lulling into a state of relaxation across his lap. His large hands move up and down, rubbing my back, smoothing over the ridges caused by my bra, and then down lower to coast over the lines of my underwear.

I brace for embarrassment, but it doesn't come. There's

only contentment as his hands grasp my ass, then massage it with wide palms.

"Talk to me." Ellis's voice is smooth, even toned as his ministrations never stutter. "What stressed you out today? What made you come here tonight?"

My eyes flutter before slipping shut as I breathe in and out, my fingers twisting against the soft sheets. "Work." I breathe in and out, focusing on the feeling of his hands digging into the muscles of my hips, then my lower back. "It's always work. Sometimes it's family too — but mostly it's work. There's a huge project coming and there's this *guy* —" I cut myself off, struggling as my mind spins, before the dam just *breaks*. "He's such an asshole. He never steps up, and he never does his job. He's the son of someone on the board, so they overlook everything and he had the *audacity* to walk into my office today and drop a packet of unorganized shit on my desk. He said he was going on vacation and would look over it before he presented it to our top marketing client — and —"

I have to take a breath again as my shoulders shake, anger and disappointment in myself mixing into a volatile cocktail in my veins. Ellis's hands move to my shoulders, rubbing them gently until I can finish speaking.

"And then he just smiled and said, '*be a sweetheart and handle this for me.*' I was so shocked, I didn't say anything as he walked back out."

Ellis's hands keep me grounded as I work through the emotions rising into the back of my throat. "I'm doing this before I feel out of control, Ellis. And it sucks because I know I'll end up doing the project for him, like I always do, but he'll get the credit, like he always does."

The sight of my coworker's smug face makes me want to claw up the sheets in rage, the frustration bubbling up even hours later. If only I had a fucking spine to tell him no, or throw the papers in the trash. Ellis's hands move from my shoulders until they come to rest on the curves of my hips, then they leave my body.

I lift my head, turning partially to look at him, just in time to watch his right hand come down with a *CRACK* against my bare thigh.

Gasping, I flinch away from him, brought back to reality in an instant as the pain fades as quick as it came. His palm covers the stinging skin, fingertips soothing the sharpness. Ellis stares down at me, raising a single eyebrow. "You won't do the work for him."

"What?"

He raises his hand again and I tense a half a second before it cracks against my right thigh. My legs clench in his lap as my mouth drops open, eyes locked on him as his expression never changes.

"Say it. Say, *'I won't do the project for him.'* Right now, fragola."

Swallowing the lump in my throat, I shiver at the feeling of his palm on my right thigh. "I won't do the project for him."

"Good girl," Ellis purrs, his hand leaving my thighs as he rubs my back again, massaging out the tension. My heart spikes again as I brace for another spank, but nothing comes as I chew on my lip and look back again.

"Say it again. Louder this time."

His hand strikes my left thigh again and I arch into the impact instead of away from it. A cloying wave of pleasure and pain washes over me as I gasp, "I won't do the project for him."

Murmurs of praise about how well I'm doing, how good I am, how *strong* I am, rain from Ellis's lips as he gently rubs the stinging skin. I turn my head away from him and let it hang down to the bed as I breathe in and out, my shoulders shaking. His hand smacks my right thigh again, making me jolt as my thighs clench. Biting the tip of my tongue, I fight back a moan at the pang of arousal shooting straight to my clit.

"Say it, Ines."

"I won't finish the project for him," I whine as the pads of his fingers brush over the sensitive skin.

"Color?"

His palms cup the insides of my thighs, squeezing. "Still green." Sighing, I relax into him as his hands massage my inner thighs, forcing my clenching muscles apart as my eyes roll into the back of my head. I sound half drunk as I moan, "That feels so nice."

"Does it?" I don't need to see his face to know he's smiling as one hand skirts up and down my exposed legs. "Can I flip your dress up, Ines?" When I nod, he pauses with a hand on my hip. "Verbal answers, please."

"Oh." I turn my head slightly, looking up at him with a little smile. "Yes, you can lift my dress, Ellis." I feel a giggle build in my chest as he growls softly, sending another vibration through us both. His fingers toy with the fabric before he slowly pulls it up the backs of my thighs. My forehead hits the sheets as I arch my back, breathing out when I feel the coolness of the room brush over my exposed ass and underwear.

I took care to put on something nicer before I came here tonight — just a pair of black bikini panties — but when Ellis pauses, I know he's staring down at me.

One finger runs along the line cutting across my asscheek. Biting my lip, I peek up at him, my breathing stuttering out at his expression. Ellis's eyes are mostly black pupil, focused on my skin, the gold a bright border around them as he huffs out a breath of his own. Before I can look away, his gaze flickers to mine, a dangerous smile lifting his lips.

"Did you soak your little panties after four spanks, fragola?"

A moan slips out, soft and wanton as I press into his touch. "Yes." My clit throbs as he smiles at me, running his hand over my ass.

"You are *such* a good girl. You listen so well."

Preening under the praise, I feel myself blush as I stare up at him, transfixed.

"I would normally make you count your spanks as punishment." His hand moves, straying between my thighs to barely graze my underwear before pulling back as his voice grows rougher. "But you've been *so good*, haven't you? You need to be rewarded, not punished. Do you want me to reward you, fragola?"

"Yes, please." Squirming in his lap, I stretch out even farther, arching my back to knock my hips up into the air. "Reward me, Ellis. I've been a good girl."

His laugh goes straight to my cunt as he grabs my underwear with a growl. "I'm going to pull these ruined panties to the side and see how wet you are. Give me a color."

"Green!" I squeak as he follows through on his promise, exposing my pussy to him as he rips my underwear to the side, leaving them cutting into me as he glides his knuckles between my thighs. Choking on a moan, I press my head against the bed. The shame at how wet I am, somehow makes this even hotter as I whimper, "Touch me, *please*, fuck, *please* —" My toes curl as he spreads my arousal, then uses two fingers to open me to him. I shiver, shaking in his lap for a moment as he doesn't move, just breathes out harshly as he stares at me.

"*Fuck*," Ellis finally curses as my clit throbs. He inhales deeply, a growl in his chest echoing through the room as his fingers slip against me. "You smell like berries — just so fucking *sweet*."

Whining, I bite my tongue as his thumb slides down, ghosting over my swollen clit. "You're so wet. You want me to touch you, Ines? You want me to rub this needy little clit until you soak my lap? I said I would reward you, but do you really deserve it when you were about to get off on me spanking you?"

His taunts crawl under my skin as I writhe into his touch, trying to get the friction I need as his thumb presses down on my clit. I sob unintelligibly, rocking into him.

"Answer me, Ines. Be a good girl."

"Touch me." Turning my head to stare at him wide-eyed, I plead, "Please finger fuck me, touch me, eat me out, hit and spank me, pull my hair, *fuck* me — do *anything*. I'm yours, Ellis, I'm *yours*."

He snarls, then flicks my clit with his thumb. I grab onto the sheets with a cry as I feel his slick fingers rub against my entrance. His whole hand between my thighs moves with each rub until he presses firmly against my clit, working me up harder.

Gasping, I come off the bed and almost off his lap, hoping the room is soundproof as I'm reduced to shaking and sobbing at the feeling of him forcing my orgasm to the surface. It barrels closer and closer — then he pulls his hand away. My neck jerks as I turn to curse at him just as his hand comes down hard in a *SMACK* across my pussy.

The pain radiates across my oversensitive clit and instead of cursing at him, I let out a string of obscenities into the sheets as I wiggle in his lap. His other hand grasps the back of my neck, pinning me in place as his right hand continues to smack my clit, over and over again. Shockwaves of pleasure radiate through me as my toes curl. My cunt clenches around nothing as a feral moan claws its way out of my chest.

He stops after ten smacks in a row, leaving me shaking as I feel the wetness seep from between my legs. My head spins as I breathe heavily — I didn't orgasm — but it feels like a feather's touch could send me spiraling as my body tries to reconcile the pleasure humming through me.

"Color?"

"Green." I rear up easily, shoving his hand off my neck as I catch him off guard. Ellis's eyebrows shoot to his hairline as rational thought flies out of my mind. "Oh my god, it's *green*." Spinning, I straddle his lap, feeling the hard length of him settle between my thighs with my dress rucked up between us as I grab his face and drag his lips to mine. His shock only lasts a moment before he kisses me hungrily, our breath mingling as I pant and dig my fingers into his long hair to cling to him.

His hands fall to grab at my sides, dragging me closer as I grind down against his erection. The thickness of it makes me shiver as our foreheads meet, rubbing myself against him over and over again as my shoulders shake. "Fuck, I'm sorry," I gasp as I kiss him again, fingers twisting in his hair. "I should have asked before kissing you."

He laughs against my lips, pulling me even closer as our bodies grind together. "It's okay, Ines. Everything is okay." One hand raises, then pushes my red hair from my face as Ellis looks up at me with a soft smile. "I made you too impatient, sweetness. You did so well."

Humming, I lean back into him as our noses brush and I stroke his mussed hair. One of his hands braces against my lower back as he kisses me again, slower this time, like he's savoring the movement of our lips. His tongue darts out and I part my lips while carding my fingers through his hair.

A low purr rises in his chest as I untangle his hair, leaning fully against his chest. Ellis's lips shift to graze my jaw, then dip lower, sucking at my pulse as he tongues the skin there.

"Can I mark you?" he groans, grinding our hips together again. "I'd love to leave you covered in my love bites, Ines. You look so pretty when your skin is red."

"Your handprints are already on my thighs." Pulling back just enough to stare at him, I bite my lower lip. "You might as well put them on my ass too while you mark the rest of me up."

His growl makes me shiver as he buries his head in my throat, sucking on the skin just above my jugular. I gasp as he bites down hard enough to hurt, but not enough to break skin. Pressing my hips against him with a shudder, I bare my neck to him. The feeling makes my blood heat as I grind down harder, chasing a slow build of an orgasm. His hips jolt up, and I swear I feel him convulse a little as he grunts.

"You taste so fucking good." He snarls the words in my ear, giving the other side of my neck the same attention by fisting my hair and jerking my head to the other side. "Smell so fucking good too. I know your little pussy wants to come, Ines, but not yet."

One hand holds my hips, stopping me from continuing to rock into him. He drags himself away from my throat, pushing me back a little. "Stand up for me. Take your clothes off."

It takes every ounce of my self control to stand up on shaking legs. He looks a mess on the edge of the bed, his hair down and tousled, with a visible wet spot on his crotch. Pressing my lips together, I tug my dress down over my hips partially, flushing. "Was that me?"

Ellis looks down at himself, a slow smile on his lips. "Not all of it. I came a little when I bit you. Hard not to."

Shoving my hair out of my face, I laugh, looking down at my heels. "Oh."

"Strip for me." I look up as Ellis shifts on the bed, leaning forward to watch as I grab onto the hem of my dress. Pulling it over my head, I let it drop to the floor in a pile, just in my bra and underwear, which is still pulled to the side, exposing me. His gaze flickers down, his shoulders flexing as he breathes in.

"Everything except the heels..." One of his thumbs runs over his lower lip and I stare as he licks it.

My nipples harden as the cool air caresses them. Dropping my bra on top of my dress, I lift a leg and shimmy my underwear off, standing still as Ellis eyes me. He stands slowly, stalking forward until my breath catches when he drops to one knee. His hands smooth over the fronts of my thighs, then pick up my right leg. Resting my foot on his leg, Ellis's large fingers deftly undo the buckle of my heel before slipping it off my foot. My mouth goes dry as he massages the arch of my foot before repeating the process with my other shoe.

"There we go." He looks up at me from his position on the floor. "I'm exactly where I want to be, Ines. Doesn't that make you feel powerful?"

He's right. Standing above him, stark naked, while he kneels in supplication fully clothed — it *does* make me feel powerful. Breathing out, I reach for him, making him rise to stand in front of me before pulling him down. Our lips clash as his hands splay across my back, fingers finding the divots in my skin left by my bra. He soothes them with gentle touch as I back him toward the bed.

"Can I put a blindfold on you, fragola? I'd like to try something."

"Yes." I miss his fingers as he pulls away to open the cabinet I saw earlier. Hanging inside are various toys and tools, including a flog and paddle. He ignores them in favor of grabbing a silk blindfold from a drawer. Flashing me a smile, Ellis shuts the cabinet and walks back over, this time standing behind me.

The silk runs across my shoulders as he kisses the back of my head. Hands appear in front of my face as he lifts the blindfold, pulling it across my vision before tying it securely.

"I'm going to guide you to the bed." Ellis kisses a shoulder. "Then you're going to get on all fours for me."

His hand takes mine as the rest of my senses go into overdrive, trying to make up for my sudden blindness. I trust him as he helps me crawl onto the bed, his hands only wandering slightly to frame my hips as I bend down. The moment I feel him move away, my heart rate kicks up again.

"Give me a color, sweetness."

His voice comes from the other side of me, and I turn my head toward it, discombobulated as I suck in a ragged breath. I want to say green — to agree that this is fine — but anxiety crawls up my throat as I clasp at the sheets.

"Y-yellow."

His soft footsteps are quick as he touches my face. The feeling of his hands on me soothes the fear immediately as I lean into him. "Talk to me. Do you want me to take the blindfold off? Is it too much?"

"No." I breathe a little easier as his hands cup my jaw. "I just want you. I just like feeling you — I like it when you touch me, when you're around me."

He chuckles, a gentle sound as his nose brushes mine. The kiss he leaves on my lips is sweet. "I just need to take my clothes off, sweetness. Let me tell you everything I'm doing. How does that sound?"

I feel slightly embarrassed as I nod, turning to follow the sound as he moves away again. "I do want to see you eventually."

Ellis laughs again. "You will. I promise, but you are both completely in control right now and you're trusting my choices, right?" The bed moves under my hands as a metallic *click* reverberates through the room. "I just moved a bar into place above your head on the bed frame." His hand travels down my calves before he's gone again. "Now I'm standing up to take my shirt off." The rustle of fabric hits the floor as I breathe in, wondering what the bar is for.

"I love watching you right now." His voice lowers. "You're being so good listening and waiting for me. You remember my tattoos from earlier? You haven't seen them all yet, but you will." His belt clinks just before he pulls down the zipper of his jeans. "And now I'm going to take off my jeans. They're soaked with both of us. I'll have to do laundry when I get home later, but I may just delay it. Only so I can keep your scent on me for a little longer."

I flush, breathing a little harder, and flinch when there's a *thump*.

Ellis curses. "My boots just ended up across the room. It was very ungraceful — I'm glad you didn't see that."

I laugh, hanging my head as I hear him shift to take off the rest of his clothes now that his shoes are off. The thought of him standing just to the side of me, fully naked, makes my heart tighten in my chest.

"Ellis." I breathe his name, hearing him walk to the bed. "Get the fuck over here and touch me."

The bed dips with his weight as he laughs. His hands smooth over my legs, seeming to touch me all over before he kisses my neck. I turn into the touch, breathing hard as he bends over me from behind. Reaching a hand back, I find his hair and hold his head against me as my legs shake. Ellis pulls away for half a second before he knocks my stance wider.

I gasp as he cups me with a hand, pressing his palm against my clit.

"I'm getting under you." He releases me before I feel him partially scoot under me. My head spins as his hands grasp my sides, lifting and moving me exactly where he wants me until I can feel his warmth under my body, my legs spread wide to stay kneeling on top of him.

Ellis's hands grasp my thighs, then pull me down. My ass hits his chest, not his legs, and I shake my head, breathing hard as I realize I'm almost sitting on his face.

"I want to taste you," he purrs as he forces me to sit down. "I haven't stopped thinking about wrapping my lips around this little clit."

I moan, the mental image of his head between my thighs making goosebumps rise on my arms. My hands fall, holding his face as I fight against his grip to hover. "I'm going to crush you."

"No," he growls, "you're not." One hand on my hip moves to my wrists, grabbing both and lifting them. I frown, reaching up until my fingers catch on the cold metal bar above me. My lips part as Ellis hums. "There you go, grab on, Ines." His hand drops back and while I'm distracted with grabbing onto the bar, he seats me fully on his face.

Gasping, I cling to the cool metal, moaning as his tongue darts out immediately to taste. He licks up my pussy before burying his face in me, movements quick and precise as he sucks my clit between his lips, guiding my hips to grind onto his face. My thighs *will* suffocate him, but I don't care as I cry out, clinging to the bar with both hands as I grind down in sharp, quick circles. The ruined orgasms from before come back full force as his tongue thrusts up into me, his hands angling my hips so he can reach every inch of me.

My thighs shake as he moans. One of his hands grabs my ass, kneading it as his tongue slides in and out of me, his nose nudging my clit. My core clenches as I curse, dropping a hand to grab at his hair, shoving him against me as I ride his face. His tongue lavishes me as my muscles tense, my body curling forward. It's only the bar above me that keeps me upright as I grit my teeth, at the very edge.

"That's it." Ellis's voice is muffled as his hand moves from my ass only to smack it. I jolt, clenching on his tongue as he switches again to suck on my clit.

"Don't stop." I push his head against me, feeling flushed all over. "Fuck — do *not* stop." My other hand drops from the bar, grabbing onto his head as my back arches. He flicks my clit with his tongue, the roughness of it sending me into overdrive as I shiver. Bowing forward, my core clenches as my orgasm hits hard. I come with a scream of his name. His tongue moves from my clit to my pussy, humming and sucking with a satisfied groan as I ride his face through the end of my climax.

Before my brain can wrap around what just happened, he grabs my thighs and flips us over. My back hits the bed, eyes suddenly blinking rapidly as Ellis rips the blindfold off. His hand cups my jaw, tugging me against him as he kisses me heatedly. I moan, tasting myself on his lips, letting him devour me as his large body covers mine. My eyes slip shut when his hand pulls my hips open for him to settle between my legs, lifting one of my legs to wrap around his waist.

Pressing my palms against his chest, I breathe hard as I look up at him, our lips sliding apart. Up close the tattoos are all a blur of color, some kind of family crest above his heart, wings over his upper arms, and even more scattered across his gold skin. My fingers curl against him as my throat goes dry.

He taps my chin to lift it. "You can look all you want later, Ines. Right now though, I want to fuck you." Ellis leans in, kissing my jaw as he whispers, "Can I please fuck you?"

Nodding into his touch, I slide my hands around to clasp the back of his neck. "Only if you promise to spank me again."

He grins, kissing me roughly as he pulls my hips up. Kneeling on the bed, he holds my lower body higher than my chest, staring down at my bare form as he grinds against me slowly. “Whatever you want, sweetness.” He lets out a shuddered moan as he rubs through me, getting slick from my earlier orgasm. “I just need you to know that my cock isn’t normal.”

I pause, breathing out as I look between my legs. His length *looks* normal, except for the little bumps that run up and down his thick cock. Ellis fists himself, looking down at me. “They’re barbs. When I come, they’ll press into you and keep me there until I empty in you.”

I had to sign a release that I was on birth control before I even stepped into the club, and I’m thankful as I stare at his thick cock, pressing my hips up against him. “I guess you should fuck me now, then maybe again later just to make sure you’re satisfied.”

Ellis groans as he falls partially on top of me, kissing me roughly as he rubs against me again. The pressure of his head against my entrance makes me whine against his lips as he pushes in slowly, each inch sinking in making my toes curl. Grabbing his hair, I pull it as he pulses forward with tiny thrusts, making my eyes roll. Ellis’s lips score across my jaw and down my throat, sucking and biting as he pulls back one last time before slamming home.

“Fuck!” I arch my leg higher on him, digging my heel into his back as he breathes out hard. He jerks inside me as I adjust to the stretch, feeling him everywhere. After a moment, he starts to thrust steadily. Digging my nails into his scalp, I cling to him as each jerk of his hips makes my body shake. I turn my head, burying my teeth where I can reach — the side of his jaw. He growls, deep and low as he starts to pound into me, making the entire bed shake as he fucks me deeply.

With every thrust, my mouth drops open wider, drawing inhuman sounds from me as I feel the little bumps on his cock ripple through me, literally ribbed for my pleasure as they stimulate my walls. The barbs catch every few thrusts, like they're threatening to dig into me, and it makes me shiver as I consider that he's going to be stuck in me until he comes enough.

Running my nails up and down his back, I drop my forehead to his shoulder, clenching around him at the thought. Whining, I grind against him, thrusting back onto him harshly. "*Fuck*, I'm going to come."

He drops a hand between us, finding my clit. Rolling it between two fingers, he thrusts faster until I arch into him, screaming as I press my face against his chest and come so hard everything goes quiet for a moment. His fingers don't stop as he groans, the bed shaking harder as he pounds into me. "That's it, sweetness. I know you have more." He lifts my hips higher, giving one last slam before he pulls out. My eyes drop to his soaked dick before he flips me over to my stomach and thrusts back in from behind.

My head drops to the bed, my gasp muffled by the soft sheets as his hips slap against mine. The sound is obscene, skin hitting skin until one of his palms comes down to slap the side of my ass.

I clench around him again, writhing against the bed as I feel my lips part, choking on my own pleasure as he fucks me through the end of my orgasm and into another one.

He does it again, spanking me so hard I see stars. His hands grasp at my hips, manipulating and harshly grasping at the stinging skin as I unravel around him again, ass up and chest on the bed.

Ellis curses above me as his hips slow, pumping in steady bursts as he breathes hard. "Last chance, fragola. If I don't pull out now, I'm going to come in you and my barbs will keep us together until I'm done." I feel drunk as I cling to the bed, pressing my ass back against him. He laughs, but it's strained. "Just give me a color, baby. I'll take it from here."

I wish we had hand motions as I turn my head to slur, "Green. I want you to come. What will make you come?"

He blows out a breath behind me, then moves. Ellis's body covers mine, almost impossibly large as he pins me down to the mattress entirely, our hips pressed together as he kisses the shell of my ear, his voice a growl. "This. I'm going to fuck you so hard you can't think, and while I do, I'm going to turn your pretty little ass so strawberry red you can't sit for a week. Do you have another orgasm to give me while I use you to get myself off? Can I have it, please?"

One of his hands shoves between my body and the bed, pushing my hips up just a hair so he has room to pull back and pound into me. The angle makes my eyes cross as I press my face into the bed, completely at his mercy while I just nod and cry out. The ridges on his cock stroke deeper, growing larger as they start to rub rhythmically against my g-spot. My legs shake as he fucks me into the mattress with a snarl.

"Good girl." Ellis grabs my hair in a fist. My heart rises to my throat as I feel his pace stutter, one hand coming down to spank across my ass. "Again." He pulls back, rocking into me as he smacks me again, making my pussy clench against him as he repeats it twice more on each side, leaving me shaking under him.

His hand under us finds my clit, and the second he rubs it I'm gone. Spit flies from my mouth as I scream into the bed, coming around him as my entire body gives out. He holds onto me as his hips slam into me once, twice, before the barbs suddenly dig into my inner walls. There's a brief stab of pain, before it's replaced with pure pleasure as his cock jerks and I feel the warmth of his cum flooding me.

Ellis's lips score across the backs of my shoulders as he

groans and growls, sounding like an animal as he ruts into me from behind, before he buries his teeth into my shoulder again, holding on as his hips rock with little jerks. My head spins as he just *keeps coming*, until I feel it start to leak out of me, the bed growing wet under us.

He finally slumps forward, one hand on the bed near my head as he struggles to hold himself up, breathing hard. "Good girl. Good girl, Ines. Such a good girl for me." He kisses my shoulder where he bit me, then pulls back, the barbs contracting to allow him to slide out of me with a wet sound.

I lie there boneless on my stomach for a moment, truly fucked stupid as I steady my breathing. He stumbles off the bed and I reach for him, turning my head to watch as he walks over to the sink, pulling out a pair of washcloths from the under cabinet before wetting them with warm water. As Ellis comes back over, he guides me to roll over, then bends between my legs, lovingly wiping up the mess, before using the second washcloth to press the warmth between my thighs.

Sighing at the feeling, I sink against a pillow, my eyes slipping shut as I feel him bend to kiss my stomach. "The barbs have a mild anesthetic, but if you need human pain medicine, I have some. I'm sterile, so you don't need to worry about your birth control not working."

Something about the statement makes me giggle as I reach for him again. He finally abandons the washcloths on the floor before letting me pull him down on top of me again. Tilting my head up, I kiss him slowly, focusing on pushing his hair out of his face as he settles against me. The weight of him is so welcome, it feels normal and comforting, like this isn't the first time we've been together. Even though I know it was our first time — I don't want it to be the last.

As he kisses me gently, his hands work down my body, rubbing my sides, then my hips, then massaging my inner thighs. It's mildly arousing, but mostly relaxing as I breathe against his lips. He pauses as he moves up to my full breasts, muttering, "I should have given these more attention. Next time." He kisses my jaw as I smile.

We finally settle with him lying next to me, my head on his chest as I run my fingers over the ink. His fingers move through my hair, untangling portions of it.

"I promised that I would make you feel good. Did I?"

My skin tingles as I tilt my head to look up at him. "Yes."

"Good." Ellis's smile makes my stomach flip. "You can fall asleep for a few hours. I'll wake you up in a bit and get you a car home."

Humming, I adjust my head on his chest, my eyes closing as I listen to the purr rumbling throughout his chest, deep and contented. The sound lulls me into a sleep that overtakes my entire body, dragging me under.

I step into the office, clad in pants and a high-neck blouse to hide the sheer amount of marks he left on me. The receptionist smiles brightly, leaning over her desk to call after me, "You got a delivery! They're on your desk!"

A brief burst of hope flares as I pocket my phone. Ellis didn't send a single text after I gave him my number last night — but I know immediately why as I open my office door to a huge bouquet of lilies. I step over to them in a trance, noticing a small box and a note, which I pick up first.

You won't finish the project for him. Be ready at six, fragola. – Ellis

My heart flutters as I read the note a second time, before opening the lid to the box.

Six chocolate covered strawberries sit inside. I pluck one from the box and bite into it, the sweetness sliding down my tongue with a promise of what's to come later.

CURE FOR LONELINESS

THE BOOK LOOKS PRETTY normal on my grimoire stand, except for the fact it's smoking red mist that's quickly filling the room. That definitely wasn't listed as one of the spell's after effects. Waving a hand over my face, I cough as I clear enough of the magical pollution to see the final part of the incantation.

The candles flicker at the edges of my pentagram as I raise both hands above my head and finish the chant in Latin, only slightly butchering the pronunciation. But it's almost there and sometimes *almost* works good enough for a summoning spell.

Red light fills the room in a flash, before it fades. In the center of the ritual space, a being kneels. Their shoulders are slightly pointed, cobalt blue ram horns curling down from their head to touch skin of the same color at their jawline.

"Who summons me? What soul seeks damnation?" Their voice reverberates through the room, but as they stand, I glance at the book in confusion.

"Uh..." I hesitate before stepping toward the podium, trying to clear the rest of the smoke to stare at the pages. The devotion spell is there — the one I prepped for and laid out all the supplies. There's only one slight issue, instead of *eternal devotion*, like I *thought* I read, the font actually reads *eternal damnation*.

Whoops.

The demon turns to watch me with endless black eyes. "Witch?"

"I made a mistake." Holding up a hand, I flip back and forth, trying to figure out if I just fucked up the spell or if I really misread the entire summoning concept. Damnation is... not what I was going for.

Frantically flipping back and forth reveals nothing. The demon stands there quietly before muttering, "What kind of mistake?"

Biting my tongue, I look back at them before rubbing my nose. The smoke lingers in the air as I nervously look between the demon and the book. "Well... I was — I mean — Okay, so maybe you'll laugh at this! I don't have anyone to damn, let alone myself. I..." Trailing off, I avoid their eyes, pressing my lips together. "I wanted to summon a friend."

"A friend?"

Slowly, I look up at the demon, waiting for laughter, or scorn, or *something*. I'm pretty used to people immediately retorting with some kind of snide comment. This wouldn't be the first time I've fucked up a spell. Instead, the only sound in the room is the quiet crackling of the still lit candles.

"I thought the spell was summoning devotion, not damnation." Closing the book, I push up the sleeves of my shirt, starting the process of cleaning up my own mess. "I'm sorry for taking you out of hell. I can dismiss you if you need me to." Some demons can freely walk between the sub-dimensions and the mortal plane, but others have minor powers and need to be returned. I've never done it myself — my magic has never been that successful, unlike literally everyone else in my family — but I could try.

The demon steps past the candles with ease. My head snaps to watch as they bend to snuff them out. "I can be summoned but not contained, don't worry witch."

"Oh." With my hands on the book, I slide it from the podium and then hold it out to them. "I found this in my family's library."

The demon looks down at the worn cover, a flicker of a smile gracing their features before taking it from me. "Ah. I know this one." Turning it this way and that, I watch as they thumb through it before holding it back out to me. "Keep it. I'm Easohn of the seventh realm."

"Lucy." I smother out another candle, pushing my blonde hair out of my face as I clear up the bundles of herbs that I didn't burn. Easohn bends to help, moving behind me as I carry the unused supplies to the small cabinet I keep in the sitting area connected to my room. Our manor is quite large — but the family has been practicing for generations, and that amount of time tends to translate to not only powerful sorcerers but also generational wealth. The endless well of great magical power seems to have skipped a generation in my case.

"It's a pleasure to meet you, Lucy." Easohn pauses next to the cabinet, before tilting their horns toward the chalk pentagram. "Can I help?"

Picking up a spare rag, I spray some cleaning solution on it before offering it to them. Easohn joins me as I bend down and scrub up the chalk, careful of the wood floors. As we move around each other, I clear my throat. "Do you... do a lot of damnations?"

"Some." They meet me in the middle, before taking my rag and walking it over to the hamper next to the cabinet.

Brushing my hands off, I stand and watch as they turn around and survey the room. "So, what would you like to do?"

I clasp my hands together in front of myself, rocking back and forth on my heels. "Well... I don't have a task for you? I don't have anyone to damn —"

Easohn waves a clawed hand at me. "Not important. What were you going to do with the companion you summoned?"

"Oh!" Turning on a dime, I rush over to the coffee table in front of the fireplace. The sitting area is just large enough for a couch and TV pushed near the fire, leaving extra room behind it for spells and summoning circles. Picking up a platter, I turn sharply with a smile, holding it out to Easohn. "I made cookies! I thought it would be nice to watch a movie with them. Or you. If you have the time. Even if you don't, you can still have a cookie."

Their gait is slow as they walk toward me, giving me a moment to take in their slender form, clad in a neutral swath of fabric acting as both shirt and pants. It's much like what I've seen other demons wear. I think the princes of hell dress quite fancy, but I've never met them face to face. I know my brothers have, but somehow my mother has always made sure I'm not in the room for those meetings.

Taking a cookie, Easohn bites into it before motioning to the couch. "Then we will watch a movie."

I have to slam my mouth shut to suppress my smile as I put the cookies back on the coffee table, spinning around the couch to collect pillows and blankets as Easohn settles into one side of it. I cover them up without asking, nudging a pillow under their feet resting on the table, before grabbing the remote and collapsing next to them, curling up against their side.

"I'm going to put on one of my *favorites* and if you don't like it, I can change it."

"If it's your favorite, then we'll watch it." They pull me closer, then carefully make sure the blanket covers my lap. It's kind of sweet, really.

Hitting play, I reach forward and grab a cookie for myself, letting the chocolate chips melt on my tongue as I hum happily. "I like this one because I think a lot of movies about witches kind of get it wrong." Something about Easohn makes it easy to talk as I stare up at the screen. There's a young girl on screen, getting her first broom and heading out on her own. My heart warms as the animation lights up the screen. "I think it's nice that she tries and wants to help. This isn't how normal magical families operate. We train privately, and then your parents pair you with a family or being who buys your loyalty and magical usage. That's why I like this one. She might not get it right all the time, but who does, you know?"

My voice goes quiet at the end as a pang of hurt travels through my chest.

Easohn raises a hand before gently placing it over mine in my lap. "Can I ask why you have to summon someone to do this with you, Lucy?"

My throat tightens as I glance up at them. With no pupil or iris, I can see myself in the reflection of their black eyes. Tears prick at the edges of my vision as I force a smile. "Well, don't you ever feel lonely?"

They pause, before tipping their chin slightly. "Occasionally. There is a lot happening in hell, sometimes time to myself is pleasant."

A lump forms at the back of my throat, sitting heavy as I feel Easohn's hand gently tighten on my own.

"But that doesn't mean I don't understand loneliness. Is that what you are?"

"Yes." With the admission, the tears well and I pull my hand away to wipe at my eyes. "Everyone is always busy. My brothers are working with very powerful people now. My mother casts spells for the governor, and my father works with warlocks across the world. I… I'm not on their same level." Suddenly the house around us feels vast as I try to focus on the movie instead of the growing pain of speaking. "I don't really have any friends, Easohn. It's just me. I don't think my family has friends either, just people who see them as useful as long as they have power, but I *don't* have power and I guess that means I don't deserve friends —"

Easohn cuts me off, moving on the couch to touch my chin with a claw. They tip my face up to look at me seriously. "Never say that again. You don't have to do anything to earn a friendship. Understand?"

Sniffling, I nod as I wipe my eyes. "They were going to marry me off."

Their head tilts, eyes narrowing.

"I… don't like people like that." Glancing away from them, I feel their claw slip away from my face. "I don't know if I've known someone well enough to like them that way." It's not the first time I've said the words, but instead of falling on deaf ears or eliciting a horrified response from my mother, Easohn stays quiet.

I'm not childish. Not like she's always said. I may enjoy childlike things, but I refuse to age and suddenly disregard everything I've ever enjoyed in life. What would be the point of that? I also won't let her marry me to someone, magical or non-magical, to place me in some gilded cage away from the rest of the family. My magic might not be as fine-tuned as theirs, but I do have things I *want* for myself. Is that not allowed?

"Does that make me broken?" I look back at them, grasping for their hand, clinging to them. "Are there other people or demons who don't like people in that way? Am I wrong?"

"No, Lucy." Easohn's tone is gentle. "You aren't broken, or wrong. You are just you, and that is enough."

The tightness in my chest eases as I stare at them. "Thank you."

They smile before squeezing my hand. "Tell me why you enjoy this one so much."

I curl back against their side, my fingers threaded with theirs as I explain the plot as things happen. When the movie is near its end, Easohn pulls me closer and puts on another similar to it. We must sit there for hours, because in the morning I wake up with the blanket over me and the demon gone.

My eyes land on a note by the empty cookie platter.

Lucy,

I look forward to your next summons. Call for me anytime.

Your friend, E

MORNING ROUTINE

YOU HAVE A MATCH!

I highly doubt it.

The subway jostles me into the person crammed next to me, but neither of us flinch as the entire car just moves with the wave. It's easier to roll with it than try to combat the awkward nudges and bumps. I'd be more concerned if it wasn't a gargoyle — he looks no older than forty, which probably means he's closer to six hundred, and he doesn't even glance at my phone as I open TITAN to see who the algorithm has put me with this time.

Three nights ago, in an *admittedly* slightly wine drunk haze, I agreed to the app's terms of services. Then I immediately activated the free trial for a month that was "guaranteed to find you your monster match, or your first month's subscription is also free!"

Sighing, I stare down at the alien on the screen. His bio clarifies he's from off-planet, along with his pronouns and the fact he's "not looking for anything serious" and that alone makes my eyes roll even though he's kind of cute. Still, I hit the big red button to reject him and then pocket my phone.

The gargoyle next to me raises a stony eyebrow. My cheeks heat to a thousand degrees as the subway screeches to a halt at my stop and I duck around him to get away, knowing he definitely just saw me, a plain old human, eyeing monsters on a dating app.

What he *doesn't* know, I try to remind myself, is that I've tried them all. I've been on the hook-up apps, the sugar daddy and sugar mommy apps, the "just here to make friends" apps that are actually hook-up apps, and the highly niche apps for farmers, or celebrities, or even hopeless women in their thirties who are tired of being single.

Sucking in a breath, I linger at a corner, waiting for the signal so I can cross with the rest of the bodies around me. I made a move to the city after years of lingering in my small town, just doing work that paid me, but wasn't very fulfilling. Since I've been here, it's felt like a rat-race... but an almost pleasant one. I love seeing so many different people and species every day, and I found a really great position with a start-up that lets me work from anywhere.

Which is why I feel a shiver of happiness as the bell overhead rings. The coffee shop smells like pumpkin and cocoa, remnants of the holiday season lingering in the air as I join the line. I scoped out a few places after moving, but this particular shop quickly solidified itself as my favorite. It's become my morning routine to stop by.

It has three levels — most people climb all the way to the top to tuck themselves into a quiet corner, but I like the handful of tables near the register. I can hear the din of others' conversations and watch the crowds walk past the window in between work.

The human man in front of me yaps into his phone, talking

about deals and dividends as I bounce on the balls of my feet. As he steps up to order, I peek around him.

Standing behind the counter is an orc, easily seven feet tall, with black hair pulled into a bun on the top of his head and tusks coming out of the front of his face. I've never seen an orc with his coloring. Instead of a mossy green, he's almost emerald, and in one ear a ruby earring catches the light. He smiles wide at the man in front of me, tattooed hands moving to take the cash from him before handing over the man's change. As the human moves to the pick-up counter, I step up, still feeling warmth in my cheeks.

"There you are!" The orc grins, busying himself with finishing up writing the man's order on a cup before turning his full attention to me. His name tag tilts to one side, but I don't need it — his name was burned into my mind the first time I walked in and saw him.

"Hi, Immon." Smiling softly, I glance up at the menu like I've not been here a thousand times.

"I've been testing out a few new syrups from home." He leans toward me and I catch a whiff of the coffee and musk scent clinging to his skin. "Want to try an elderberry scone with a new latte on me?"

Fumbling with my wallet, I stare up at him. "Oh no, you don't have to —"

"No, let me." Immon smiles. "Anything for my best customer, Hanna."

The flush that works its way up my body has to be ridiculous, because the way he says my name has my heart pounding like I've just run three marathons. Immon waves me away with another smile, pushing his glasses up on his nose. "Go grab your favorite table before someone else takes it. I'll have it out in a few."

"Okay." The word is barely a squeak as I turn obediently

and head toward the table near the front window that no one else seems to like sitting at. It's kind of squished between two other tables, but it isn't a bad place at all to sit for hours. There is a little draft though, which is why I made sure to wear one of my warmer blouses as I unpack my laptop from my bag and chew on the inside of my cheek.

Immon talks candidly with another customer, laughing and pointing out things on the menu as I glance back at the counter. The line dwindles and he grabs the fairy who's often here to take over on register for him. Just as I turn to glance at my laptop after it boots up, I catch his eye. Immon points to a plate as he drops a fresh, steaming scone onto it and then holds up a finger to signal that he'll be by in a minute with my latte.

I *try* to focus on opening the company messaging system and getting my programs up, but my heart races as he approaches my table, placing the plate and coffee right next to me. The side of Immon's mouth lifts a little as he looks down at me with a sheepish look.

"I really hope you like this, which is why it's on the house. If you don't, just let me know. The syrup I used is gnarlerberry, I had to source it from some old clan members in Scotland." Reaching up, his bicep flexes as he ruffles his hair, sending his bun askew. "Totally safe for human consumption and all that. I try to be mindful and mark anything that's a species specialty on our menu, but this one seemed like it would be good for spring?"

As he rambles, I pull the latte closer to me and inhale. The smell is like a mix of mint and blackberry and I hum as I lift it to my lips, blowing carefully before taking a sip. It glides down my throat like butter, a pungent mix of herbal and sweet, with a hint of vanilla from the oat milk that Immon used.

His cheeks are a darker green when I look up at him and nod rapidly. “That’s *very* good, Immon.”

His grin splits his face, making his tusks gleam as he nods back at me. “Good. Great. Flag me down if you need anything else. Are you sticking around for a while?”

The question catches me off guard as I look back at my laptop briefly. There’s no reason to go home early today — I’m still debugging the test version of the app I’m helping to code for the launch. This beta version is being concurrently worked on by myself and a team of three others, and all of us work at odd hours. I seem to be the only one who’s alive before eight in the morning, and while it’s nice to log in and see a ton of work done, I also have to go behind them and fix mistakes made at three in the morning while they were blitzed on energy drinks.

“I think so.” Looking back up at Immon, I fidget a little. “Is... that okay?”

“Oh yeah!” He rushes to assure me, brown eyes widening. “I just thought I’d bring you lunch too, y’know if you’re still here?” He rubs the back of his neck again, cheeks darkening as someone calls his name from behind the counter. He hesitates, looking down at me. “If I still see you working in a few hours, you’ll eat again.”

I open my mouth to protest, certain he doesn’t mean he’ll comp *another* meal, but then he nods once to himself, like the decision is non-negotiable and strides off.

Sitting at the table, I stare at my laptop for a solid minute, mind reeling. It’s *unfair* how attractive he is — tattooed all over with a pair of glasses perched on the bridge of his nose. His tusks are always a bright pearlescent white, shiny under the cafe lights. Glancing over my shoulder at the counter, I watch Immon guide his fairy coworker through making a specialty drink for a naga waiting at the register.

The naga turns, his snake lower half curling around

multiple tables and chairs as he makes his way to the table near mine, where there's a bench instead of a traditional chair. He slithers up onto it, coiling partially as his human upper half puts his own laptop and phone down on the table's surface. His scales are so blue, they almost look like gemstones shining in the light.

Catching my eye, he gives me a pleasant smile. "Sorry, you weren't holding this table, were you?"

"No!" I feel myself flush. "No, just delaying starting work."

The naga rolls his eyes sympathetically. "I completely understand. Let me guess... accounting?"

"Coding." I laugh softly, shifting in my chair so I can speak to him a little easier. "You?"

"Law." The naga extends a tanned hand to me. As I shake it, I let myself take in his face. He's very angular, with a sharp jaw, but kind, round eyes and a broad nose. "I'm Alec."

"Hanna." Taking my hand back, I nod at my screen, smiling. "Good luck with your work."

"You too, Hanna." Alec's eyes linger on me for a moment before we both turn to our respective laptops. Something about the feeling of his eyes sticking on me for an extra heartbeat makes my stomach flutter.

Forcing myself to focus on my laptop, I slip my headphones in, reopening the logs from last night to scan the work completed while I was asleep. The latte goes down smoothly as I switch between drinking it and munching on the scone while I mindlessly fix minor mistakes before reaching the area that I've been fine-tuning; the user's view of one of the app menus. Digging into work, I keep my head down, responding to a few messages and emails, until my phone buzzes gently on the table next to me.

I look down at it, almost not registering the notification, before I flinch, grabbing it quickly. I open TITAN, praying Alec didn't see it from so close to me as I look down at the minotaur's profile. He's in finance, with a mottled white fur pattern that looks aged, but distinguished. I linger on his profile information for a moment, skimming the details. When I signed up for the free trial, it did warn me that they would be using their algorithm to constantly scan active profiles and send them as matches, but this is the first one that's caught my eye.

Something makes me turn my screen off as I look up, staring out the window to watch people pass by on the street outside. A small part of me can't stand the thought of burning through the options on yet another app. The romantic in me wanted to ask out Immon *immediately* after I moved to town, but I hesitated too long.

Two and a half months ago, I came in and sat down immediately because I had to respond to an email. While I was typing up a quick reply, I heard Immon's warm laugh behind me and turned only to see him and another orc leaning against each other, losing it over something on her phone.

Ever since then I've seen her around a handful of times. They're clearly close, even though they've never kissed, it's not exactly like there's been an opportunity for him to lay one on her considering this is his place of work that he's busy running. She's stunning — of course — taller than he is, with cool green skin and warm chestnut brown hair that's always perfectly curled. The tip of one of her tusks even has a little hole drilled in it to allow for her to thread a gold ring through it.

I *tried* not to be jealous, but four days ago I walked in to order and he was standing behind the counter. In the middle of greeting me, he lit up with a smile brighter than high-beam headlights and rushed around the counter to hug her tightly. It shouldn't have bothered me — I'm a *customer* for fuck's sake, but the sting lingered in my head so long I gave up working after only a few hours and skulked back to my apartment to hole up in my room and avoid my two roommates.

Then I got wine-drunk and downloaded TITAN.

This morning though, he'd seemed so earnest. Giving me free coffee *and* my favorite pastry? Who the fuck did he think he was?

"Hey, Hanna?"

Jerking slightly at the sound of my name just loud enough to break through my earbuds, I turn, taking one out to look at Alec.

He smiles again, his eyes darting from my headphones to my face. "I'm sorry to bother you. You looked like you were thinking about something, but I wanted to do this before I leave." Alec slides forward, then places a napkin next to my laptop with his name and number on it. "I don't do this often, but I'd really like to see you again, and I knew the likelihood of us running into each other in the coffee shop again would be slim in a city this big." He shrugs his shoulders, his smile softening. "You can throw it away, or save it, but I'd like to get to know you if you're open."

"Oh." Blinking like an idiot, I look at the napkin and then stare up at him, my mouth dropping open a little wider as he packs up his laptop and then holds his phone.

Alec hesitates, like he wants to say something else, then lets out a breath. "I know that dating a naga might be different for you, as a human, but—"

"Oh, god." I wave my hands at him, coming back to my senses. "No! No, please don't think I'm hung up on that. I'm just not all here today." I can feel the heat radiating off my face as I try to come up with an excuse why I'm being so *weird*. This is it. This is my chance to see someone who seems *real* and earnest for once. Pulling my phone into my hand, I open it and key in his number in front of him, sending a quick text. "There, now you have my number."

Alec's eyes widen, before a smile splits his face. He nods as his phone dings in his hand. "Okay. Yeah, great." He leans back, the smile still brightening his features. "I have to go into the office, but — uh — we'll talk."

"Yeah." I give him a soft smile back, my hand landing on the napkin. "It was nice to meet you, Alec."

He casts me another surprised, yet pleased look, before he nods and slithers from the cafe. My heart feels like it's going to race out of my chest as I slip the napkin off the table and look down at it. Alec's handwriting is a looping scrawl, somehow soft but sharp at the same time.

I *could* see myself going out with him, but...

My chest smarts as I put the napkin safely into my laptop bag, rubbing the back of my neck. Out of nowhere, I feel a burning guilt. Is it misleading to have the app on my phone and to be hung up on a coffee shop owner who's clearly already in a relationship with someone? Am I even in the right headspace to date someone right now?

"Hungry?"

Immon appears out of nowhere, making me jump. His brow is tight as he stares down at me, head slightly inclined.

"I saw you finished your scone and drink." Picking up the empty plate and mug, his knuckles flex slightly. "What were you and Alec talking about?"

"You know him?"

"He works for my father's firm." Immon's eyes somehow look ten times darker as he towers over me. The thing is, butterflies erupt in my body at how *possessive* he looks in the moment. "I split off and opened up this place when I realized law wasn't for me."

I have no idea what to say, and just as I open my mouth to

try to come up with something coherent, my phone buzzes. My blood runs cold as Immon's eyes flicker to the screen before I can. His expression darkens and I turn slowly to see TITAN with a reminder to respond to my latest match.

A naga, a minotaur, and an orc all in one day.

Immon turns, his voice rough. "I'm getting you a sandwich."

"What?" I flinch when my phone buzzes again, this time a text from Alec following up the dating app notification.

Immon looks like smoke is about to plume from his ears and mouth. If he were a dragon — maybe it would — I've never actually met one. "I. Am. Making. You. A. Sandwich." After he grinds out every word, he turns on a dime, stalking behind the counter and then slamming the door open to the kitchen.

I stare, bewildered, as it swings on the double hinge. The fairy behind the counter eyes me, her wings fluttering nervously as she finishes taking an order. The cafe has emptied a bit since it's a few hours after lunch rush. I look back at my phone in alarm that I sat here this long without realizing, before rubbing my eyes.

Picking up my phone, I silence TITAN from notifying me any more today, unable to stomach swiping yes on the minotaur match. That leaves me staring at the text from Alec — it's utterly mundane — just about how he'd much rather work from the cafe than his office.

The same smarting pain lights up in my chest again and I press my lips together as I put my phone back in my bag, turning to watch as Immon emerges from the kitchen. The *platter* he's carrying isn't just a sandwich. It's a whole goddamn spread as he strides past the counter, straight to me to put it down. Yes, there's a hot, pressed panini on the plate, with what looks like ham and a myriad of fresh toppings with a thick spread that smells like aioli — but there's also multiple sides, including fresh fries, steaming hot chocolate chip cookies, and mixed vegetables in a dressing.

"I can't eat all this." Moving my laptop in alarm, I shove it in my bag.

Immon pushes the plate in front of me and then drops into a seat he drags right next to mine.

"Hanna."

"Immon —"

"*Hanna.*"

Startled, I focus on him as he leans closer to me.

"I am only going to say this once. Eat your lunch. Clean your plate. Finish your work for the day. But don't you dare leave this cafe when it's closing time. You and I need to talk."

My lips part, and my heart skips a beat as I mumble, "But why? You're seeing someone."

Immon's eyebrows raise to his hairline. "Excuse me?"

"Uh —" I scramble, cursing myself as he just waits. "The woman who was here a few days ago. Brown hair. You left me in the middle of ordering to hug her."

He blinks once, then twice, before a delighted spark of mirth lights up his eyes. "You mean my *cousin*, Kaelari? Who just scored a modeling job for fashion week as the first orc to walk the runway?"

Oh shit.

Shame and embarrassment clog up my throat as we stare at each other. Immon stands, putting the chair back in its place before pointing at the food. "Eat, Hanna. We'll talk about this in an hour."

For some reason, I turn to the spread and obey him, eating it slowly as my mind screeches like a banshee about my own stupidity. Every single time we've chatted, joked, slowly gotten on a first name basis flashes through my mind — he learned my *order*, he started bringing all my food to my *table* — I've been so blinded by the fact he could be seeing someone else that every little sign I was hoping for just slipped right past my radar.

Everything is delicious, down to the serving of vegetables that I polish off last. When I reopen my laptop, I finalize the next version of the internal menu and close out for the day since the rest of the office takes odd hours all the time. Then I shut my laptop and wait.

A few stragglers mill in and out of the coffee shop. Some of the people from the tables upstairs climb down as it nears closing, tossing goodbyes to the fairy worker as she cleans up the espresso machine and takes multiple bins of dishes to the back. My skin prickles as I wait, my heartbeat slowly but surely getting faster as the fairy finally leaves, closely followed by two people from the kitchen that I've never seen before.

As the bell dings, Immon emerges from the back. His shoulders pull back, keeping his stride straight as he locks up, then turns to me, standing in the middle of the room.

"You stayed."

"You asked."

His lips twitch. "I think that was, unfortunately, more of a command." A slight sheepish expression crosses his features. "Sorry."

My cheeks heat slightly. "I liked it."

We stare at each other, uncertain of the next move before he steps over, offering me a hand. "Come with me?"

As I take his hand, Immon scoops up the strap of my bag, then guides me behind the counter and through a door. It takes us down a hallway, then to a back staircase. I glance at him, and he nods upward with a hesitant smile. "I also live here. I'm on the fourth floor. If you don't want to walk, I can carry you."

I choke a little, laughing as I start up the stairs in front of him. “I’m good, thanks. Though I might have to use my inhaler at the top. I have shitty lungs.”

The heat rolling off of him just steps behind me makes me feel a bit dizzy as we climb. “That’s fine. You take my breath away too, Hanna.” A shiver of something salacious crawls up my spine at his words.

As we reach the top foyer, I suck in a labored breath. Immon already has my bag open for me. I fish out my inhaler from the little pocket I keep it in, using it once, then twice, before exhaling as I tuck it away. His free hand lifts, just barely brushing my cheek before he seems to force himself to pull away and unlock the door. I follow him obediently, desperately curious as I kick off my boots next to a pile of his shoes just across the threshold.

I don’t know why I expected brick and industrial decor, because that’s not at all how the cafe is styled downstairs. Instead, his apartment is very classic, with deep and rich brown walls, framed with intricate wood detailing that signal the age of the building. As we walk down a short hall, he carefully props my bag in a chair and then clears his throat.

“I’m going to change out of my work clothes. I smell like coffee beans and food —”

“I don’t mind!” I cut him off, my throat catching. “I like it.”

Immon’s expression softens. “I mind. And I need to get something from my office. The living room is through that archway. Make yourself at home.”

Nodding, I watch him retreat down the hall before stepping through the arch and taking in the open space. There’s an open stretch of wall that leads to his kitchen, with dark blue cabinetry and brassy accents, but it’s the huge arched window overlooking the street below that draws me closer.

No wonder he took the top floor — while the ceilings are

lower than the rest of the building, it gives it a warm, intimate feel. The afternoon light is already fading, casting everything in an almost-orange glow that makes the entire place feel magical. It's a good reminder that there *is* magic in the world, while humans and non-humans alike go about their lives below. I'm at a point in my life where I get to witness the meshing in this place, sustaining myself with a job that I'm mostly happy to do from anywhere I want.

Footsteps behind me make the hair raise on the back of my neck. Immon comes into the room, having exchanged his henley and jeans from before for a casual pair of gray sweats and a blue t-shirt that's tight across his upper arms and shoulders. He walks right up to me, a small leather-bound book in his hand that pulls my focus.

"It's something my father gave me a few years ago when I went off on my own," Immon supplies, holding the book out to me. "Orcs are very familial-focused. We love each other and our extended family members deeply and dearly, but we also value when the children want to forge their own paths. Some people thought I'd take my law degree and follow in his footsteps, but he was just happy to see me pursue what I loved."

I take the book carefully, glancing down at the cover. "*The Orcish Guide to Courting?*"

With one hand on my back, Immon guides me to a soft white sofa. "When a child leaves their parents, it's customary for them to receive a parting gift. Traditional families will include money, a weapon with the family crest, and a courting book that has remained in the family for generations. This one was my father's, given to him by his parents. Most orcs understand that the three gifts are symbolic — money to know their family will always be their first supporters, a weapon to carry the family with them as a sign of protection, and the book that contains not only the Orcish ways of courting, but family histories of past couples."

I flip open the cover, seeing just how old the paper is. As I thumb through the first few pages, my eyes skim the handwritten words. Instructions filter in slowly — you must get to know your intended partner, make them comfortable in shared spaces, and feed them. My heart rises in my throat as I reach pages upon pages of handwritten accounts of Immon's family members recounting the first meetings with their own partners.

My eyes are burning by the time I look up at him, feeling truly dumbstruck as I whisper, "This whole time?"

Immon's smile is gentle. "The whole time."

"I —" Flustered, I shut the book, blinking back the moisture in my eyes. "I had no idea. If I had —"

"It's okay," Immon soothes me immediately, covering my hands with his own. He gazes at me, his voice deepening. "I should have made my intentions clear. The first day you walked in, I asked everyone I knew in the area if they'd ever seen you before — the stunning, curvy red-haired human who stole my heart at first glance. When no one knew you, I realized you'd just moved to town and I didn't want to startle you immediately with... me." He hesitates, clearing his throat. "Orcs don't date many people who aren't also Orcish. Sometimes a witch, or a shifter, but our customs are very serious, and it can come across as a bit much."

My entire body softens as I lean closer. "Immon, I liked you from the first day I saw you. I waited for months, trying to come up with something to say and the day I was going to ask you if you'd like to go out, your cousin came in and I..." Shaking my head, I sigh, looking down at our hands. "Some people may be confident enough to ask anyway, but I took it as a sign."

He's quiet as I carefully place the book on the coffee table near us, clearing my throat. "I downloaded a few apps because I was lonely, but nothing ever felt right. I kept thinking about asking you, but then I was too nervous that it was inappropriate and I didn't want to jeopardize the friendship slowly budding." Refusing to meet his eyes, I instead watch his hands. His large thumbs smooth over my wrists, not thin by human standards, but smaller than him, in proportion. "I wanted to move on. Alec gave me his number today."

"Alec should mind his own business." The ire in Immon's tone makes me look up in alarm. He scowls, not at me, but more in general. "He is *very* aware of what an orc looks like when they're courting a potential partner. He did it to enrage me, and he's lucky he slithered away before I could hang him by the tail from the rafters."

An inappropriate laugh barks out of me and I cover my mouth in shock.

Immon huffs. "He *knew* you were already spoken for."

"I didn't." Lowering my hand, I exhale softly. "Am I just oblivious?"

Moving his hands from mine, Immon cups my face gently, shaking his head as he stares at me. "No, but you *felt* it right? The little spark of ache? The trepidation? Please tell me that's why you never followed through with anyone. Please tell me you feel the *yrugrn*."

The guttural noise that leaves him is so unfamiliar it shocks me almost as much as the flare of heat in my chest. Every time I'd see someone on my phone who might be an option, I'd hesitate to swipe, or be slow with my replies, or outright ghost them after a short conversation. Each time felt heavy, like I was making the wrong call by trying to connect with someone, my gut intuition forcing me to stop. I thought it was nerves—but the way my body lights up with Immon's hands on me makes me question it all.

"What is that?"

"Old magic," he whispers as he moves closer to me on the couch. "Once the courting passes the first few stages, the prior magic built up from years of clan celebrations and holidays takes root. In pairings with two orcs, it's like..." Immon looks up for a moment, his expression growing dazed. "It's like knowing your future minutes before it happens. Everything clicks into place. I've heard witches feel it, if they commune with the old gods. Shifters too, because they're so closely tied with the earth. I thought maybe..."

"And what would it mean? If I did... feel something?"

The hope in his eyes sends another wave of emotions through me.

"I would declare my intentions." Immon's voice grows stronger as he grasps my face. "I would make it known to you and everyone around us that I have set my sights on you. As our relationship developed, so would the magic. It would work until we either parted ways, or dedicated our lives to each other. Whether that's in months, or years — it's a malleable commitment, an understanding that I am devoted to you, Hanna. I would vow to know everything about you, to make every room you enter the most welcoming space I can, and to keep you full, safe, and happy."

With one thumb stroking the apple of my cheek, Immon shifts his other hand to cradle the back of my head. "Hanna, I want to court you. Will you let me?"

I scoot closer to him, our legs knocking together on the couch as I push a strand of hair out of his face that escaped his bun during the day. Gently, I lift my other hand and slide his glasses off, before placing them to the side. His eyes squint slightly, but he must still be able to see me because he whispers, "Hanna?"

"There." I touch his jawline, tilting my chin up. "Now you can kiss me without them knocking into us."

His breath escapes him. As Immon pulls me close, he angles his head slightly to the side, making sure my face can slot between his tusks as he kisses me deeply. It sends a shiver up my spine as my eyes close, sinking into the feeling of *rightness* that floods my veins. It's like none of the rest of the missteps matter, because everything was supposed to lead to this moment, this very second where we both breathe the same air and the world feels slightly off its axis.

His nose brushes mine as his lips barely skim the side of my mouth. "I've waited for that. I've dreamed of it for months."

Goosebumps rise on my arms as I move closer to him, almost crawling into his lap. I just want to keep touching him, to keep prolonging the contact as his hands map my face and his lips keep dragging soft kisses from my own.

"Do we have to do everything else slowly?" I gasp as the coolness of a tusk slides against my cheek.

"Are you asking me if I fuck during a courtship, gorgeous?" Immon pulls away just enough so he can look down at me, eyes narrowed in concentration. "Because there's never been one before you, and I don't intend for there to be one after. I make no promises that I won't propose immediately after I get you in my bed."

The sheer concept that he's so committed makes my cheeks heat. With a little smile, I throw a leg over his, nodding at him. "You're all in, got it. Just making sure I'm not crossing any boundaries."

He groans, one hand dropping to grab a handful of my hip as my skirt rucks up. The fabric is too long to be indecent, so it pins to my body instead, trapping me from truly sitting across his lap. Immon's eyes roll as he drags me closer, then kisses me a little harder.

"Why do I feel like if I told you to take your clothes off right now, you'd do it?"

"Because I would," I breathe against his cheek as his hand on my hip slides further back, grasping at my ass. "I liked when you told me what to do in the cafe. I liked listening."

He makes an agonized sound before he stands, lifting me with him effortlessly. I squeak as one arm slips under my legs and the other goes under my back, bracing me as he turns abruptly and takes a stumbled step forward.

"Bed. Now."

Clinging to him, I bury my head in the softness of his t-shirt, snickering. "Can you even *see*? Your glasses are on the couch!"

"Fuck." Immon stops short and I clamber out of his hold, darting to grab them before handing them over. He blinks owlishly when they're back on, tilting his head down at me as he sucks in a breath. "Are you sure —"

I grab his hand, tugging him toward the archway. "I'm going to just start opening doors until I find one suitable, Immon. You better get me in your bed —" He bends down, sweeping me up again as I shriek, letting out a deranged laugh as the orc holding me charges down the hall to the final door and shoves it open.

The decor doesn't even register to me as we paw at each other. His hands go to my skirt, tugging the simple elastic down to free my legs of the floor-length material as mine drag his shirt up from his belly. There's a roundness to his torso that speaks to all the pastries he eats and I smile as I back up toward the bed, giggling as I notice the tent in his sweats.

"Get your ass on my bed." His hands drop to his waistband and I clamber up as he divests himself of them, leaving a pair of black briefs on as he stalks forward. Immon grabs one ankle and I hit the bed with a soft *oof* as he knocks me off balance, it turning into frantic giggles as he shoves at my shirt, cursing softly. "How the fuck does this work?"

"It just goes over my head! The ties on the front are decorative!"

Shoving his hands away, I tug it over my head and throw it somewhere in his room, sitting in just my bra and underwear. Somehow, it brings the situation back down to earth as Immon rests a knee on his bed and looks down at me.

"Last chance, Hanna. If this is too much, too fast, you have to tell me now because I will go out tomorrow and buy the ugliest, gaudiest Orcish courting band you've ever seen and clasp it on your wrist before breakfast."

Tilting my head at him, I grin. "It goes on my wrist? Like a bracelet?"

"Rings are too small —" Immon crawls overtop of me, his body shadowing mine as he cups my face and kisses me again, breathing hard. "Some orcs give their partners a cuff every year. They end up with arms full of them. I'll buy you rings and bracelets and whatever you want. Just let me show everyone you're only mine."

Smiling against his lips, I nod. "Okay. Sex first, jewelry later."

"Thank the gods." He practically crumbles on top of me, pinning me down with his hips as one hand braces against the bed, stopping himself from fully crushing me as the kiss quickly turns hungry. I can barely catch my breath as I pant, letting out small sounds as Immon's lips move across my jaw, then down my neck. His fingers slip under the straps of my bra, pulling them down as the coolness of his tusks make my skin prickle.

Heat builds in my belly as his lips graze the top of one breast. "You're so soft." His voice is breathy as he cups my chest with his hands, holding my breasts up before unlatching my bra in one smooth motion. They sag before Immon's hands knead them slowly, thumbs gliding over my nipples as he rests his head on my sternum for a moment, breathing harshly.

I shiver as his lips wrap around a nipple, sucking and licking at it. As his tongue rolls around the bud, my back arches from the bed. My legs splay wider, allowing him more room to settle. "Let me explore you," Immon whispers as he moves to my other breast. "Let me make this moment one you will never forget, gorgeous."

Nodding, I bite my tongue as his hands map my body with intent, like he's committing me to memory. As his green touch pauses on my stomach, I swallow, glancing down to watch his nose nudge until he reaches my belly button. I try not to fidget as he breathes out, muttering, "I've fed you well." Immon kisses the swell of my stomach, groaning. "I've provided for you and now I'm going to pleasure you."

Writhing under him, I let out a hiccuped moan as his mouth lands on my mound, working at me through my underwear. A flush spreads across my body as Immon groans, his tongue soaking my underwear as his jaw works, his tusks bracketing my pussy perfectly, like a frame.

His hands work under my hips, supporting my ass before he tugs my underwear down, shoving it off my legs and spreading me fully for him. As Immon leans up, his dark eyes take me in. "Can I do anything I want to you?"

I choke on a bit of spit as I stare up at him. "Like what?"

His thumb smoothes over the arousal already gathering near my clit, spreading it as he circles the bundle of nerves. "Like finger you, Hanna. I want to bury my fingers and my tongue in this pink pussy, and then I want to spear you with my cock until we both can't think. Then I'll probably feed you again." He looks contemplative for a moment. "Yeah, I'll fuck you nice and deep and then you can eat the dinner I'll make for us with my cum still warm in you."

Entirely bare under him, I let out a breath as his eyes meet mine.

"Yes?"

"Yes."

"Good girl." Immon bends, his back arching as he buries his face between my legs. His tusks force my thighs to remain open as his tongue immediately flattens on my clit. The pressure makes me moan as a hand works between us, teasing in and out of my entrance before he slides it in deep. The stretch makes me roll my hips forward into him. Immon's lips suction around my clit, rolling and humming as he thrusts his finger in and out, just big enough to stimulate, but not enough to really drive me crazy.

Dropping a hand to his hair, I work at it until I release his bun. Black strands thread through my fingers as I fist his long hair with one hand and use the other to divest him of his glasses again. I try to be careful when I drop them to the bed, but he nudges another finger at me and my toes curl with a surprised little groan.

His jaw works at me as he makes satisfied sounds, eating me out with enthusiasm as I sink into his bed, my eyes rolling back and forth. Immon adds his second finger until he's fully working two in and out of me. The slick sounds coming from between my thighs make me feel a bit lust-drunk as I spasm around his two fingers, grinding against his tongue.

After a moment, he pulls back enough to grunt, "You taste so fucking delicious." Immon's eyes dart up to mine as his tongue hangs out of his mouth, before he bends to give me a long lick again. "Want to come on my fingers first or my tongue, gorgeous?"

I stare at him as his fingers slide in and out. "I —" They

hook in me and my eyes cross as I jerk into him. "Oh *fuck. Immon.*"

He chuckles, then presses a hand to my stomach, holding me in place as his hand starts moving faster. The pressure on my abdomen drives me crazy as the wet sounds grow more intense. I've never come without my clit being stimulated at the same time, but he almost has me there in moments as I gasp rapidly, clinging to his hair. His head moves against my grip, growling, "That's it, baby. Pull my hair while I make you come."

Immon's fingers crook inside me, catching with each thrust and my thighs shake as I jolt on his bed, cursing loudly as the orgasm punches me in the chest. The pleasure spreads across my body as I clench around him, unraveling and pushing closer with a whimper. He lets me ride his hand through the aftershocks, eyes never leaving my face until I go limp. It's only then that he slips his fingers free and shoves his briefs down with his other hand. As his cock bobs, the light shines on something underneath it.

I stare, transfixed as he uses the hand that was in me to slick himself up partially, mostly rubbing my release on the bulbous head. Immon lifts himself to kneel between my legs as he jerks his cock a couple times, his shoulders tense. "Fuck. Have you ever been with an orc, Hanna?"

"No?" My voice barely sounds like my own as my head spins with what I'm looking at. Immon presses his cock against his belly, exposing the underside to me where a row of silver barbells pierce his dark green skin in a line. They slowly get bigger as they lead down to his heavy sack.

When my eyes find his, he looks positively ravenous. "You're going to count as each one goes in, and when they're all there, I'm going to fuck you so hard into this bed you can't walk. Then I'm going to leave you dripping in my cum — and orcs come *a lot*, gorgeous."

I'm nodding before he can even finish his thought, my hands shaking as I reach for him. "Yes, please. Come here and fuck me."

He leans back down, using a hand to hold onto my face as he kisses me heatedly. I feel him settle between my legs, the length of him landing on my thigh as I lose myself in the feeling of his touch. Immon lifts me higher on the bed with a hand on my hip, supporting my lower half by shoving a pillow underneath me. The angle makes me grind slowly against him and the barbells feel slightly chilly against my heated flesh as we both moan.

Putting a hand next to my head to hold himself up, he grabs himself before guiding his head through the wetness between my thighs. I watch as he notches at my entrance, teasing the tip inside me once, then twice. Biting my lip, I hiccup as he slides deeper on the third thrust, flopping back on the mattress as the feeling of him entering me forces all the air from my lungs.

Immon kisses my throat, staying still as I adjust. The first piercing barely teases my skin, but the drag is enough to make me whine.

"Count, Hanna."

"One." My toes curl as I lift a leg, wrapping it around his hips. The angle of the pillow and our hips colliding make a delicious combination as he thrusts deeper. "Two!"

He laughs, the sound rolling over my skin. "Four more."

Fuck.

With the roll of his hips, each barbell adds pressure to the already full feeling of his thick cock entering me. I'm sweating by the time I pant out the fifth one, my eyes crossing as Immon holds himself above me.

"Last one, gorgeous. Can you take me all the way? You already feel so good around me."

Digging my nails into the back of his neck, I crush our faces and chests together, kissing him roughly as I shove my hips against his, hissing out as I feel him sink almost to the hilt. Biting down on his lip, I gasp, "Six."

He holds onto me, giving up on bracing himself on the bed. Instead, Immon's hands lands on my hips as he forces himself to pull out, then fucks me back into the mattress by entering me fully again. The kiss could barely be considered one as we both gasp into each other's mouths, spit smearing between us as I cry out. Immon pounds into me steadily, fingers digging into the flesh of my legs as he keeps me right where he wants me.

The barbells stroke my inner walls with each movement. I'm more turned on than I ever have been as he manhandles me, tusks against my face, grip bruising me, as I start to flutter around him in no time. Immon grunts, pulling out before his hips snap into mine. "Already?"

Tears prick in my eyes from the sheer pleasure, pressure building in my stomach. "I — I can't — oh my *fucking* god —"

One of his hands rises, cupping my face and holding me gently as he stares down at me. As he fucks me harder, deeper, impossibly steady with each motion, he murmurs, "Look at you. You're drunk on my dick, aren't you?"

A shiver crawls up my spine as I stare up at him, the moisture overflowing in my eyes as my chest spasms. I start to cry as he thrusts in and out of me. Immon's brow furrows as he wipes at my cheek with a thumb, panting as he slows enough that he can grind his pelvis against my clit at the end of each meeting of our hips.

"Just let it out, gorgeous. Cry and come and do whatever you need to. You're safe. You're mine."

All the air leaves my lungs as his piercings stroke over my inner walls. The orgasm lights up every nerve ending in my body as my mouth drops open, not a single sound coming out as I convulse under him. Immon coos softly, his hips speeding up as he prolongs my orgasm. It turns unbearable as his hand slides from my face to my throat, holding the side of my head and applying a bit of pressure as he grunts, throwing his head back.

Our hips slap together as I keep coming, each unhinged thrust spinning me higher and higher until Immon shouts and stills. Heat fills me, a rush of warmth that signals his orgasm as his other hand drops to pull the hood of my clit back. With a groan, his thumb circles it, then he flicks my clit hard and fast as his hips jerk into me.

The final orgasm is blinding as I come around him for the last time. I scream, sobbing his name as everything goes black for a moment. My body doesn't even feel like my own when his hand drops away. The bed and pillow is soaked under my hips as Immon bends down, kissing me sweetly and slowly. I can feel my heartbeat in my throat as his nose grazes mine.

"Come back to me." His voice is slightly hoarse as he strokes my hair. "I've got you, Hanna. It's okay."

My chest aches as I cry, my breath sawing in and out as I twitch under him, truly and deeply untethered. Immon finally takes a moment to pull out and the rush of cum that follows splashes out onto the bed. Carefully, he wraps me in his arms, moving us from the end of the bed to the top, wrapping blankets around me as he rests his chin on the top of my head. One of his hands smoothes my hair as he cradles me to his chest. The steadiness of his heartbeat lulls me in and out of consciousness as I struggle and fail to find something to say.

I don't know how long we lie there before he rubs the back

of my neck and mutters, “Was it too much? Talk to me, sweetheart.”

Shaking my head, I burrow in closer, wrapping my arms around him until I can hold him against me by his broad shoulders. “I liked it. I like you.”

His chest moves with his exhaled breath. Immon chuckles softly, tucking the blankets closer around me as he nods and squeezes me once. “Do you prefer gold or silver?”

The question catches me off guard as I answer on instinct. “Gold.”

Immon’s fingers play with my hair as he hums. The effect is almost like a thrum through his chest, vibrating through me with contented pleasure, like something in him is already resonating through me. “Gold it is. Get some rest, gorgeous. We’ll get up in a bit and eat something.”

I smile as I tuck myself against him, pressing a soft kiss to his chest. “Will you make me coffee in the morning?” I already know I’m not going home tonight — and I can’t find it in me to care.

He tilts my chin up with a finger, his brown eyes so deep and warm as he whispers, “*Every* morning, Hanna. That’s a promise.”

BETWEEN A KNOT AND A HARD PLACE

THE SUN HANGS low in the sky as I walk along the garden path, leaves crunching underfoot. There's a chill in the air that my jacket can't seem to keep out, which makes sense for late February. Though, in all honesty, I don't get out much anymore when the sun *is* at its peak, considering Elric hates wearing his daylight ring.

He once described it to me as the same feeling of opening the door on a very hot oven. The wave of humidity rolling over his skin constantly — not able to burn him because of the magics imbued in the moonstone, but still wildly uncomfortable. I don't mind. I get out in the late hours of the day, preferring dusk anyway.

Sweeping my hair off my neck, I peer up at the waning sky. He's awake in the house, but we probably won't leave for dinner until the sun fully sets. We try to work in at least a few nights a month where we venture away from the manor and head into the nearest city to experience the blended culture of various species and humans — something Elric prefers after years of keeping to himself — but if it was up to me, I'd never leave my vampire or our bed.

"Dangerous to be a little morsel out all alone just before the sun sets, don't you think?"

I jolt, whirling around at the sound of a deep purr coming from the shadows where the garden blends into the forest surrounding the house. Heavy footsteps crunch old leaves and debris as a huge man emerges from the tree line, black hair pulled into a knot at the nape of his neck, muscles taut under a plain gray shirt and flannel.

"Harlan!" With a gasp, I abandon the path to run straight toward him, nearly tripping over an uneven brick as I throw myself at the giant werewolf with glee.

He catches me without flinching, chuckling as he lifts me so I can wrap my arms around his thick neck and hug him fully.

"Hello to you too, little snack. I wasn't expecting to see you in the sunlight." He tips his chin up and I press my cheek against his, humming in delight when the warmth from his breath skates over my skin as he scents me. His stubble is a pleasant scratch on my skin.

Slipping down to the ground, I stare up at him with a wide grin. "I thought you were still with your brother's pack. Did the play for alpha finally settle down?"

Harlan waves a giant hand in the air, rolling his eyes. "This happens every few years. Some young pup thinks they could do better and it spurns a handful of others into attempting to challenge him. James is always too polite to bite back unless it's a true challenge, but I have no issues snarling at them all to stay in line."

"You also don't have to deal with the repercussions." I roll my eyes at him, catching his hand and tugging him with me back to the gardens to continue my walk.

"Being a lone wolf has its perks, Claire." Harlan bends down, using his free arm to tuck me against his side even as I keep his hand hostage. "Like visiting my favorite eternal pain in the ass and the little human who is far too good for him."

I snort, leaning into him as we circle the rosebushes. Elric has a wood nymph gardener who loves to care for this place and keeps it in top shape. At the heart is a huge willow tree that's been on the property for hundreds of years, with a wooden bench made from Elric's first coffin. It's a lovely place to sit when the moonlight is streaming down through the branches.

"Where is he? Combing his hair again? Or did you spill rice on the floor to give him an enrichment activity? You know it's very important to keep an elderly mind sharp."

"I think he's still on a call with Aoto in Tokyo." Sliding my fingers against Harlan's, I shrug, unable to hide my grin at his joke. "They have to find time when they're both coherent enough to do business. We may go to dinner tonight, do you want to come with us?"

Harlan grunts, looking down at me before reaching for me. The roughness of his fingers against my hair sends a shiver down my spine as he tucks it behind one ear. "Your hair looks so red in this light." His lips lift, just so, at the edges before he pulls me down a side path that leads to the garden beds near the kitchen entrance. The air smells of basil and a variety of herbs, but my senses are overtaken by *him*, deep musk and earthy marl as Harlan backs me up against the ivy covered brick.

Leaning back, I stare up at him, smiling gently. "You left James's pack for another reason, didn't you?"

He boxes me in, one arm braced on the wall as his shoulders fall, a light sigh escaping. "It's nearly mating season. It was going to be a bloodbath anyway because they don't have many unmated pairs. It didn't seem right to tear someone away without the promise of a bond when they could have one by the end of spring."

Reaching up, I cup his face. The years of lines crossing his tanned skin converge around his mouth and eyes, leaving ghosts of expressions on him.

"But you'll rut alone? Harm yourself on the off chance some other wolf may find the one?"

He huffs, his eyes finding mine. The deepness of their brown is so comforting, just as much as Elric's red seems like an external representation of his love for me. Flicking Harlan's nose gently, I tease, "Bad dog. Take care of yourself for once."

His answering grin is equal parts exasperation and fondness. "Claire."

"Harlan." Running my thumbs over his jaw, I shake my head at him. "Use your words, you big grump."

He glances up for a moment at the fading light and I watch as he swallows, his brow furrowing then relaxing. After some thought, Harlan looks down at me, licking his lips. "It's been a few years since I stayed here full time. Your need for a bodyguard during the day has passed, and I have little right to ask you to pick up where we left off, or Elric for that matter, but..." He tilts his head, his nose almost brushing mine. "If you and Elric are still as *open* as you once were, I would appreciate the help through this rut."

I tip my head up, letting our noses touch as I smile softly. "Was there a question in there?"

"*Claire.*"

With a giggle, I tug him down to me, placing a gentle kiss on his lips as I nod. "Yes, Harlan. Elric and I are only open for *you*, and I'll be happy to help as I'm the one who can take a knot."

He groans and in the next second his kiss is searing enough

that it makes my toes curl in my boots. Years ago, just after Elric and I met, there was another vampire who wanted me — wanted my *blood.* It isn't rare for vampires to fight over the humans who smell the best to them, but the ones who succumb to the blood lust never give up a hunt. Harlan was the best of both worlds, simultaneously a protector in the daylight, and a prior paramour of Elric that had his unending trust.

Of course we all fell into Elric's bed together. It was inevitable.

Harlan's hot breath skates over my jaw as his head moves closer, breathing in deeply as one hand fists my hair to bare my neck to him. With his face against my throat, he lets out a contended sound, boxing me in closer to the wall. "Thank you, little morsel." With a little shiver, he pulls back, eyes darker as his body twitches. "Moon's almost up."

I glance up at the sky, relaxed against the wall with my hands on his face. "Go shift. I'll stay right here."

"You are too good for him." He surges forward, kissing me again before dragging himself away and shaking his hair out of its bun. "And me." With a parting look, he jogs off toward the trees.

Pressing a hand against my lips, I laugh as I watch him go, shaking my head slightly. I can't hear anything inside the house, but there's no way Elric isn't privy to the conversation Harlan and I just had. His supernaturally gifted hearing would have picked it up, or his nose sensing another creature in the vicinity.

Carefully, I shimmy my underwear down underneath the sweater I'm wearing as a dress, balling it up in my hand. A sharp *crack* sounds from the woods before a bone-chilling howl echoes in the night. I watch a black werewolf emerge with a snarl, covered head to toe in dense, thick fur. His back legs support him in bipedal form, wicked claws digging into the dirt as he stalks forward, brown eyes turned yellow as Harlan drinks me in. I watch as his lips pull back from his canines, voice somehow even deeper in this form.

"You're certain, little snack?"

I throw my underwear at his head, watching his arm dart out to catch it with supernatural speed. Harlan holds it to his snout and inhales, his entire body shaking as he breaks into a faster pace to get to me. Kicking my legs open with a paw, he keeps my thighs splayed as he crowds me against the wall, running his rough tongue over my throat.

"Tease."

Humming, I stretch to reach his furry ears, pulling his muzzle to my mouth in my best attempts of a kiss as his clawed paws scoop me up. His body is easily four to five times the size of mine in this form, but I've seen it before and it leaves a feeling of safety settling under my skin. Even with sharpness and violence being the purpose of this side of him, Harlan kisses me sweetly, his tongue lolling out to taste my jawline as he guides my legs to wrap around him and lines me up with his pelvis.

I moan gently, the sweater rucked up as the softness of his fur strokes over my exposed body. There's a weight too, hitting my thigh with heavy slickness as his cock slides out of the sheath that normally hides it in this form. Looking down, I reach between us, giving it a slight stroke, my thumb sliding over the tapered and flushed head as Harlan's teeth gently dig into my shoulder.

Shivering, I roll forward, pressing the head of him against myself. He does have *some* dexterity with his paws, but it's easier to slip him in with my fingers and his body shakes in relief as his hips take over, thrusting deep with one motion. My hand drops to his side, digging my nails into him as I gasp, my body bouncing as he pushes into me with a guttural moan.

"Didn't think" — Harlan's claws grab onto my hair, pulling my head back as he looks down at me with a snarl — "one cunt could feel *this* good. I'm going to rut you into ruin, little morsel, eat you up until there's nothing left for your fanged partner to feast on."

"She always has one more for me. Just like you do." Elric's voice sends chills up my spine as Harlan ruts into me at a steady pace. To the side, the kitchen door is open, and there my vampire leans, watching with hooded red eyes as I'm getting fucked against the side of our house.

Harlan turns to give Elric a wolfish grin. "We'll see." With that, he slams into me harder and I feel the base of his cock tease at my entrance. The knot is so thick, I hiccup a moan, grinding against him as I cling to his fur.

Elric watches before casually sliding a hand over the front of his trousers. His blond hair is just slightly mussed — meaning he used speed to get down here in time to see this. With deft fingers, he undoes the front of his pants and pulls himself out, wrapping his hand around his long cock before stroking it slowly.

"You know, just last month I tongue-fucked her so hard she came all over my face and started her period. Her blood tastes even sweeter when it's between her thighs."

Harlan snarls, turning his face away from Elric before lifting me higher, using me shamelessly as a sleeve for himself. It's all I can do to hold on as the sense is literally screwed out of me, nonsensical sounds escaping from my parted lips. He pulls me down hard and his knot just barely pushes against me, making my body tense on instinct as I muffle a scream, pressing my head against his furry shoulder.

He coos, shushing me gently as his hips surge back. "Not yet. You need to come first and relax to take it, but you will take it."

My hair ruffles, then suddenly the brick wall is gone behind me, replaced by a cool chest. Elric pulls me against him, unmovable as stone as his hands slide between my thighs, finding my clit to rub it rapidly.

“Allow me, Harlan. She’ll be ready soon enough.” My vampire kisses across my neck, before striking, burying his fangs in one side and taking a single drink before allowing Harlan to tug my hair and bear the bite to him. As Harlan moves faster, stuffing me fuller with each jolt of his hips, his tongue roves over the bite, a deep growl building in his chest.

My thighs shake, heart racing as Elric nips at my ear, murmuring, “Be a good pet and come so he can knot you, darling. Don’t make our wolf wait when the rut has already overtaken his senses.”

With Harlan’s tongue on my throat and Elric’s fingers rubbing so fast they feel like a buzz on my clit, I come. My scream echoes across the valley below the manor as the wolf inside of me surges forward with a snarl. Right as the spasms ease from the orgasm, his knot slots into place, a sense of pressure that makes stars burst across my eyelids. Working his hips forward in shallow thrusts, Harlan pants against me, repeatedly rutting against my g-spot.

Elric slips out from behind me, then kneels on the path, his hands cupping Harlan’s heavy sack as he massages it, leaning up to suck on them. Harlan shakes between the two of us, jerking into me until he howls. As he comes, I clench down on him again, another orgasm taking my breath away and leaving me shaking in between both of them.

Elric is stroking my hair, murmuring sweet nothings as I come back to Earth. Harlan shifts a little, holding me up with paws on my ass, claws digging into my skin.

“I’ll have to come again soon,” he grunts as Elric lets him hold me fully. “The knot won’t go down for a while.”

Elric rubs my back, kissing my jaw. “That’s fine, you’ll be his cocksleeve won’t you, darling?”

I moan, nodding as I lean into Harlan’s furry chest, feeling another surge of cum leak from his cock stuck inside me. “Just get me to bed and keep going, *please*.”

Harlan chuckles as Elric escorts us inside. The two of them talk softly, catching each other up as I fall into a space of mindless pleasure where the werewolf inside of me keeps thrusting to stay hard and the vampire beside me rids me of my clothes. I watch Elric bend down, kissing Harlan’s muzzle sweetly, as Harlan raises a paw to cup the back of Elric’s blond head. It’s enough to make my body buzz as they immediately settle back into old habits.

If it was up to me, I’d never leave our shared bed — a vampire on one side, and — if I can convince him to stay — a wolf on the other.

UNEXPECTED VISITOR

When I set out this morning, the news said it would be the *perfect* clear day to take in the scenery. With not a cloud in the sky, it was the ideal conditions to take the easy winding path up to the most popular tourist photography spot with the best view of the valley. In fact, they suggested doing it *before* this weekend. Their reasoning? It was the end of the season, there was no possible way more snow would come, and the blanket already covering everything will melt off soon, meaning the view won't be as lovely.

I may sue.

"Fucking shit fuckity — *fuck*." The last curse slips out as a squeak when my boots lose footing on the icy rocks and I go tumbling ass over tits down the small ridge. Fat snowflakes smack me in the face as I land dazed on a pile, barely three feet down, but it's enough to leave me discombobulated as I blindly search the flurries for what direction I'm supposed to go in.

Because the meteorologist was fucking *wrong*. I left this morning to sun, hiked to the peak just as a family of werewolves were leaving, and then promptly stared in horror as a storm moved in, dumping snow on everything including me.

Shivering in my coat, I reach up, touching my face. I still have the hood up, but I lost my balaclava somewhere a while ago. My fingers feel stiff in my gloves, because I chose my lighter gear to hike in — thinking it would be cold, but not *this* cold.

I know I need to get up and keep trudging toward where I think the road is — I have a better chance of finding someone, or yelling loud enough for someone to hear there, but I'm so *tired.* Lethargy drags me down as I stay seated in the cold snow for another few minutes, tipping my head to stare at the darkening sky.

I'm going to die out here.

The thought is sobering as I roll to my side and push up. I've never given up despite everything else in my life. Icy snow wedges past my gloves, working its way up my sleeves as I stumble back to my feet, trying to shake it free as my teeth chatter.

"Help!" My voice is hoarse as I cry out, giving up on figuring out the way. Choosing a direction, I trudge forward, the drifts getting larger and the blizzard making the visibility even worse. "Please help! If anyone is out there, please, I'm just human!" It's a long shot — but someone else may be close enough to hear me. A vampire can't die again, and I'll happily tap a vein in thanks if one swoops in to save me. My steps slow as I bump directly into a tree, leaning my forehead against it as I let out a delirious laugh. "Oh fuck, I am going to die just because I didn't double-check the forecast."

I think of the werewolf family as I brace against the pine tree, sinking lower until I'm sitting on the cold ground again. They left at the right time — it was a pair of parents with three young kids. One of them had a waggling tail when they waved at me from the back of their minivan. I'm glad they got back to town before this hit.

My eyes slip shut as I curl up against the base of the tree trunk, letting the snow fall where it may on me. *It'll be okay*. I just need to rest for a few minutes.

I hear the shuffling before I can peel my eyes open. There's snorting, a deep animalistic sound, before I hear heavy footsteps that shake the ground around me. Arms grab me, digging me out of half a pile of snow as I stare up at the sky deliriously. I'm not shaking anymore — maybe this is all a dream, like my body is letting me live out a rescue fantasy before I fully slip away?

There's a snarl, then a crunch. "Who's faster, you or Lawson?"

"Me." A deep rumble radiates through me as the person holds me tighter, aloft in the air but tucked into something soft.

"Then go, we'll be right behind you."

My face presses against whatever it is that's so plush. It feels like diving into a pile of warm blankets straight from the dryer and I hum as I curl up. Everything is quiet, except for air *whooshing* past my ears. Which is really weird, because I figured dying would be a pretty painful and loud affair, but maybe hypothermia is different. Though, I'm pretty sure I'm supposed to reach a point where I feel warm and want to strip off my clothes.

"No, don't take them off yet, snowflake," the voice rumbles, and then something touches my head, pressing me closer to the fluff. "We're almost home, then we'll get you warmed up."

I cling to the weird talking blanket person while my body bounces. The movement makes my limbs tingle and I find that my fingers hurt as they grip at the fabric. The noise dampens, then stops, before the air turns from frigid cold to cloying warmth. I can barely breathe as I fight against the fluff, pushing hard to escape the heat.

"Hey, hey, shh —" There's a blast of cold air and I fumble, catching glimpses of wood as I tumble from somewhere near a ceiling. "Oh shit —"

Instead of cracking my head open on the wood floor, someone else catches me. They pull me tight to their chest and hold my arms down as panic rises in my veins. I'm *cold* and it *hurts* and my heart is racing and —

"Reid, go start the big shower, don't make it too hot yet, it'll shock her system. Boone, grab blankets and put them in the dryer so they're warm when she gets out. I'm going to get her out of these wet clothes. I think she's in shock."

"Yeah, I'd be in shock too if a giant fucking Yeti nearly dropped me on my head," a southern voice drawls just before footsteps pass me.

Turning my head, I stare up at the face of a minotaur, wide-eyed. His fur is an orange-red, shaggy around his face, with wide white horns twisting away from his temple. The minotaur's eyes, though, are a soft baby blue, and he looks down at me before huffing, hands bracing me in his lap.

"Did you hit your head?" His Scottish accent is gentle as he reaches up a hand to prod at my hairline. "I'm not going to hurt you, but we need to get you warmed up as soon as possible, love."

I must have bashed my fucking skull in because I genuinely can't believe my eyes as he lifts me up into his arms bridal style and carries me to a bedroom. When he places me on the edge of the bed, my hands shake as I raise them to the buttons and zipper of my coat. He carefully pushes them away, shaking his head at me.

"Stop, I'll do it." His brow furrows as he focuses on undoing the clasps, then tears open my jacket, finding my wet sweater and then the soaked turtleneck underneath it. "Boone!"

"Yeah!" Another man comes into the room, this one looking completely normal except for the fact he's built like a world champion body builder. The hair on his head is part brown, part silver, and his brown eyes meet mine for a moment before he steps over, a frown pulling his mustache down on his upper lip. "Okay yeah, she may be in shock." He bends, kneeling next to the minotaur as he picks up my hands and rubs them between his own. "I'm going to trust you can understand us right now and know we're not going to hurt you, but I'm Boone. The guy undressing you is Lawson."

I stare at him for a solid moment, unable to make my voice work as Lawson — the minotaur — takes my pants off.

In the next second, Boone lifts me up in only my underwear. The air feels frigid on my skin as my teeth start to chatter and he hauls ass through another door into a steam-filled room. Inside a man towers — clad head to toe in dense white fur that is slightly curly. He looks over at me, then his eyes go to Boone before he steps to the side, allowing Boone to carry me straight into a shower.

The water hits my skin and I hiss, clinging to the man holding me. It *hurts* even though it's barely lukewarm. Boone makes a distressed grunt before he shifts me, then drops down to sit on the tile floor, holding me in his lap as he lets the water drench us both, rubbing his hands up and down my arms, then my back, and rocking me back and forth. The yeti sticks a hand in, adjusting the temperature a little higher every few minutes until I start to feel the shaking abate, my body slowly adjusting back to normal.

Every ounce of energy leaves me, like a huge wave crashing over my head as I lean into Boone, deciding he can't be that bad if he kept his clothes on while holding me.

"I'm getting the blankets, Reid. Keep an eye on them and grab some towels." Lawson leaves after poking his head in to look at us. Then it's just me in the steamy space with a towering yeti half-in, half-out of the shower, while I sit on his friend's lap.

Turning to look at Boone, I feel water drip over my face as I swallow hard, trying to clear my throat. What comes out is a croak fit for a frog, and his expression grows even more worried as he looks over at Reid.

"Just leave the towels on the bench or something and maybe go get her warm tea. You okay with that?" He turns to look back at me, hands still rubbing over my shoulders. "You aren't allergic to just some tea right?"

I shake my head and he grunts, nodding back at Reid. "Go on then, I'll get her dried off."

My throat feels like sandpaper as he stands back up, letting me lean on him while the spray drenches me from head to toe one last time. He turns it off, his shirt and jeans completely soaked as he steps out and grabs two huge towels. Using one to dry me off, he exchanges it for the unused one, only to drape around me like a cloak.

"Okay." Boone pushes his hair back, the silver catching in the light. "Now you can't stay in wet underwear, so don't take this as anything but what it is, but you need to get those off for me right now while I strip and we'll put the clothes in the wash. Lawson should be back soon with something for you to wear. Can you take them off?" He pauses, eyeing me. "Or, do you — uh — need help?"

I shake my head at him firmly, taking a step back as I pull the towel closer. He breathes out a sigh of relief, then puts his back to me, tugging his shirt over his head. I stare at his broad back for a moment as his muscles ripple under his skin. Whatever he is — he isn't human — because he has a ton of body hair and scars all over. Boone's head turns and he catches me looking as his hands drop to his jeans, raising an eyebrow.

"Alright, little miss, you'll have to pay if you want a show."

I flush, turning away to face the shower as I keep the towel draped over my shoulders, bending down to wiggle out of my underwear first. It gives me a great view of my own mottled skin — loose in some places, full and curvy in others — I'm not short or small, but these three have made me feel positively waifish in the short time I've been here.

It takes a little skill to get my wet bra off and it makes an ungodly *plop* as it hits the tile floor. Wrapping the towel tightly around myself, I peek over my shoulder to see Boone standing with another towel slung around his hips, waiting for me with his eyes on the ceiling.

"You done?"

I open my mouth again, making a sad croaking noise that kind of sounds like an affirmation. It's enough for his head to tilt down as he pushes off the countertop and strides toward me. I freeze like a deer in headlights the second his hand wraps around the front of my throat, caught between a flash of arousal and fear that mix together into a *very bad* combination.

Boone looks down at me, but instead of squeezing, his fingers massage the sides of my throat on one side, then move to the other, his warm palm easing the twinge of pain. "I think once we get that tea in you, you'll be able to speak again. We heard you yelling, the cold probably made the strain worse."

I barely nod my head, and he smiles just a little. "Come on, then." Without warning, he bends down and picks me up, towel and all. I make a choked squeaking sound as he carries me out of the bathroom and back to the bedroom just as Lawson strides through the door. In his arms are piles of actual blankets — not Reid, the Yeti — and I feel how warm they are when he nears us and drops them onto the bed. Boone places me down next to them as the two of them work in tandem. Boone opens a dresser, rifling through it as Lawson takes clothes from him and turns on a dime to me. His hooves are black and shiny as they click on the floor, and when he crouches slightly to tap my bare foot, I stare down at him in alarm.

"Just socks first." He holds up a pair of oversized wool socks and I lift my foot, letting him slip them on me. Then he shakes out a pair of boxers that look like shorts, offering them to me. "These okay?"

I nod, slipping a hand out to take them.

To the side of us, Boone is somehow already dressed again, in a pair of plaid pajama pants and a henley. He strides across the room and grabs one of Lawson's horns, dragging him upright.

"Let her dress herself, she's got her mobility back at least. We need to talk with Reid in the kitchen."

I stare open-mouthed as Boone pulls Lawson by the horn out of the room, letting the door slam shut behind them both. Alone in the room, I can finally sit for a moment to embrace the absolute gravity and insanity of the situation. It makes a strangled laugh bubble up, before I feel tears drip down my face just as fast. I've always been overly emotional, but the fear of almost dying feels like an acceptable panic to let myself embrace wholeheartedly. I cry as I let the towel fall, tugging on the pair of boxers before finding an oversized shirt emblazoned with some kind of sports logo. Pulling that on too, I go over to the dresser, hunting through it on my own until I find a sweatshirt big enough to fit two of me in the very bottom drawer. With it covering me, I finally wrap my arms around myself and stumble over to the blankets, barely moving them before I curl up in a ball at the center of the pile with one over me.

The heat is intense, but nice as I press my head against the fabric, breathing in the smell of detergent and something else muskier. It could be any one of them — maybe even the scent of all three of them — but I don't have the energy to care as I wipe at my eyes again, taking little shuddering breaths.

There's a click as someone opens the door, and I don't bother to raise my head as I hear footsteps. The bed dips next to my impenetrable pile of warm blankets before the one closest to my head moves slightly.

Reid peers over them at me, blinking slow brown eyes. The fur comes up to his face, but it's slightly thinner around his eyes, nose, and mouth. He looks almost human. As he holds a mug out to me, it makes a new round of fresh tears well.

"I made you tea. I'm sorry I dropped you." His voice is just as deep as before. A frown pulls at his wide mouth. "I thought I had you, but your jacket was slippery."

I free a hand, shuffling slightly in my pile to lean up. Reid watches me before he grabs a pillow and slips it behind my back, allowing me to sit. After I'm situated, he allows me to take the mug. It's the perfect temperature as I bring it to my lips and take a hesitant sip.

"It's only black tea." He sits with his hands in his lap. "And some honey and lemon for your throat. We may have cough drops. I'll see if I can find some."

When he moves to stand, my other hand darts out and I catch his furred forearm. Reid freezes, looking down at my hand on his arm before he slowly sits back down. Taking another drink, I try to go faster, letting it coat my throat enough so I can croak out a raw, "Thank you."

He stares at me, his eyes widening. "You can talk." Reid

glances at the door, then looks back at me. "I think you've terrified Lawson and Boone. They were fighting over how to get you to a hospital."

I clutch the mug in one hand, shaking my head rapidly as I clear my throat. "No doctors." Doctors mean hospitals with records who could put my name in a system, and that's the *last* thing I need right now.

Reid reaches out, one of his hands covering mine on his arm. My body trembles as he holds onto me. "Okay, no doctors."

Draining the rest of the mug of tea, I offer it back to him, determined now to give the other two a piece of my mind. I shove blankets to the side, scrambling out of the warm pile as I scrape my hair back, shoving it away from my face. Reid watches me the entire time, then stands with me as soon as my socked feet hit the ground.

I tilt my head, looking up at him. He's easily near eight feet, which is hard for my brain to wrap around because it's two and a half feet taller than me. Standing with my empty mug, he looks back at me, hesitating when I do.

"Where to, snowflake?"

"Kitchen." I grumble the single word before shoving the door open and making my way down the long hallway. There's wood *everywhere* — floor to ceiling, along with huge windows that take up an entire wall of the cabin I'm in, looking directly out into the worst blizzard I've ever seen. Snow drifts pile near the windows, tall enough that they make some of the pine trees outside look more like bushes. It stops my heart to think I was out in that — that I'd almost been *stuck* there.

Inhaling shakily, I round a corner to a huge chef's kitchen where Boone and Lawson are hunched over the island, arguing with their faces close together.

"No doctors." My voice sounds a little firmer, but still

husky, and it makes them both jump. Reid comes up behind me, scooting around just to refill my mug from a yellow teapot and squeeze lemon juice into it.

Boone turns, raising an eyebrow. “Now you *cannot* expect us to let you walk back out in that storm without knowing you’re going to get checked out.”

I stomp my foot, glaring at him. “I said *no*.”

Lawson raises his hands, swinging his head around to eye Reid as the yeti calmly brings the refilled mug to me, placing it on the counter next to me.

“Drink more.” Reid pats my shoulder, then moves to stand near some barstools, equidistant between myself and the two other men.

I grab the mug and take another huge swig, scowling at Boone over the rim. “I’m fine.” Gritting the words out, I clear my throat again, waving a hand at him that barely pokes out from the sweatshirt hanging down to my knees. “I just need my clothes and I’ll be out of your hair.”

“Absolutely not.” It’s Lawson who speaks this time, his Scottish accent sharp. “There is a freak storm outside and you’re only human, per your brief shout.”

“Which we’re lucky we fucking *heard*,” Boone snarls. I jump a little at the vitriol in his tone, taking a step back. “Because you gave up, didn’t you? You were just going to lie down against that tree and let yourself freeze. The only reason we were out there is because Reid keeps the emergency radio on during storms and the ranger station said a single hiker hadn’t returned. Stupid decisions — seems like you’re great at them.”

I nearly fling the mug of hot liquid at his skull, but Reid moves first, putting a hand on mine to force me to put it back on the counter.

“There is *no* reason to scold her.” He gives Boone a sharp

look. "We are all species who can handle this cold and as far as I know, the news said it was a lovely day for a hike."

"Lovely day to freeze your ass off," Boone huffs, crossing his arms.

I scowl at him. "Sorry my stupidity enrages you. Thanks for saving me. Can I have my clothes so I can get the *fuck* out of here?"

Lawson sighs. "Everyone take a breath. No one is going out in this — the only one who *could* is Reid because he's genetically built for a storm this bad. I have no visibility and Boone, you'd get turned around before reaching the main road. Now —" He looks back at me, tilting his chin down. "What's your name? We're going to be stuck here for at least the weekend, you might as well tell us."

Just as I open my mouth to tell him to shove it — every light in the cabin sparks and then goes dark. Instead of making a witty retort, I yelp like an injured dog, reaching for the counter near me to cling to it.

"Fuck," Boone curses as I hear Lawson's hooves on the floor.

Someone touches me and I shriek, pulling away immediately just to have the counter dig into my hip painfully.

"It's me — it's me, it's okay." Lawson's hands move over the sweatshirt covering my arms. My heart pounds as I sense him getting closer again, only for him to carefully pull me into an embrace. "We all have scotopic vision. Reid is going outside to check the breaker and see if it can be flipped. Boone will light the fireplace."

Sucking in a breath, I let him hold me, too afraid of the dark to move as I wrap one hand around his upper arm. Lawson rubs my back with a hand while the other guides us away from the counter. It's so dark inside everything feels oppressive and my throat starts to close as my eyes burn.

"Are there flashlights?" I stumble over the words, using him as my only anchor until there's a flare of light from the corner. A spark later and a fireplace lights up in a blaze, Boone kneeling in front of it with soot on his hands. It casts enough light to see the living room I breezed past earlier, with its huge wall of windows. There's a couch big enough for an army, along with an oversized reading chair off to the side.

Boone rises after poking the fire one more time. A door shuts somewhere and Reid comes out of a side room with snow still in his fur. "No luck. I think the grid is down from this storm." He looks down at me, frowning. "Oh, are you crying again? It's okay, snowflake, it's just lights."

I smear my hands over my face, sucking in a ragged breath. I *hate* that my default is instant tears, because my chest smarts the moment I try to suppress them. Next to me, Lawson rubs my back gently, his voice softer. "Please just come sit by the fire, love."

I let him lead me to the couch, because what else am I going to do? All the fight dies as I sit down, staring at Boone as he stands in front of the fire, the flickering light casting him in a haloed glow.

"What's your name then, little miss?" He raises an eyebrow as I watch Reid take a seat in the oversized chair.

"Lily." I miss the mug, if for nothing else but to have something to do with my hands. Even the admission feels like too much, and I look away from them all, staring at the huge windows. "It's Lily and you're right. I shouldn't have hiked alone. I was *trying* to get back to civilization, but I fell, and then it was too hard to see or move, so I *did* give up." The words leave me in a rush, feeling lightheaded and nauseated as I confess to it all. "Because the other option was making it to a hospital where someone will figure out who I am and then they'll contact my ex and if he shows up I'm screwed —

because they wouldn't validate my restraining order and he never gives up."

Wringing my hands together in my lap, I hiccup back tears, my shoulders shaking. "He never fucking gives up."

The air in the room shifts from concern to determination as Lawson touches my knee, lowering to the couch next to me. "Then there will be absolutely no doctors. No one knows you're here, do they?"

I shake my head, turning to look at Reid. "I just wanted a vacation. I just wanted somewhere he'd never think to look."

Reid's eyes narrow. "And he will never know you're here. I'm going to tell the ranger the bare minimum so they don't send search and rescue or medical." As he strides back to the other room he just came from, Boone slowly walks from the fireplace to the couch.

I avoid looking at him when he sits down near me.

"I'm a bear, Lily," he finally grumbles. "Both for making you so uncomfortable, and literally. My mom is a Kodiak shifter from Alaska and my father is a Polar from the same area, just a little north. I'm sorry." When I do finally look at him, he twists the end of his mustache, shaking his head at me. "There's no excuse, I just didn't want you to actually be hurt and not seen."

Sniffling, I wipe at my nose. "It's okay. You meant well."

"He's a stubborn bastard," Lawson mutters, then leans into me slightly, nudging my shoulder. "At least you didn't lose any fingers or toes in this entire ordeal."

I cast him a wane smile. "Can I ask what the hell the three of you are doing in a cabin together?"

Reid steps back into the room just as I finish my question. He opens the fridge without care, fishing out a drink for himself before walking over and plopping down on the other side of Boone. "We're partners."

That shocks me speechless for a moment as I look between the three of them. A yeti, a minotaur, and a bear shifter feels like the start of a very bad joke, not a throuple. Boone shrugs his shoulders at me. "He's not lying to you. We met in college. Lawson went on to become an architect and built this place, Reid's been retired from special forces for..." He trails off, squinting.

"Fifteen years," Reid finally supplies, and at my silence, he takes a sip of soda. "Yeti age slower than humans. I'm older than I appear, snowflake. I was on my third degree by the time I met them."

His nickname for me makes me blush as I focus on Boone. "And what do you do?"

Boone smiles at me slowly, rubbing his jaw. "Well a little of this, a little of that."

"He keeps bees during spring and then sells the honey at markets," Lawson supplies, leaning back against the couch with a wide grin. "And he specially made the bottles so they're little hybrid bears just like him."

"Shut up," Boone growls, reaching around me to shove at Lawson's shoulder.

I watch as Lawson dissolves into laughter, holding onto his chest. It brings a little smile to my face as Boone turns away from him, staring at Reid. "Now I just sound like *Winnie the Pooh*."

Reid shrugs, a smile creeping across his features, showing the hint of fangs. The expression makes my heart stop for all the wrong reasons, because he really *is* handsome. His jaw is so sharp, along with the tips of his ears, almost fae-like save for the fur. But even I find that charming, especially with how curly it is around his shoulders and bare torso. His lower half has been covered this entire time with a loose pair of pants that I'm now more certain than ever is for my benefit, not for Lawson's or Boone's.

The fire crackles as I look between all three of them. Reid catches my eye on the other side of Boone, then grabs him by his hair, fisting the brown and silver strands before dragging Boone against him. Reid kisses him firmly, once, making sure to bite at Boone's lower lip before releasing him.

It's all the permission my body needs to heat slightly. Boone leans back, flustered as he clears his throat.

"It's the only surefire way to shut him up." Lawson speaks behind me, making me jump slightly as I turn to look at the minotaur. He lounges back against the cushions for a moment, dressed similarly to Boone, save for the fact that his pajama shirt is just a plain tee.

"I think it would be wise if we all slept out here tonight near the fire." Reid brushes off his pants as he stands. "I'll go get the blankets. Boone, help me with the pillows?" As the two of them walk around the large couch and head down the hallway, I eye the darkness warily.

Lawson moves one leg, leaving a hoof between us. I look down at it curiously for a moment, twisting toward him on the couch.

"Have you ever met a minotaur, Lily?"

I shiver. My name in his Scottish accent is *dangerous*. Shaking my head, I reach a hand out, glancing up at him. He nods toward his hoof.

"Go ahead. It feels like any other bovine. I don't have as sensitive of nerve endings there as a human or shifter. Though my mother was human." I feel him watching me as I run a finger over the shining front of his hoof. It doesn't move under my touch, so I peer closer, tilting my head at the way his ankle angles back to his inverted knee, which supports his human upper torso. I assume there's the same red-orange fur on his lower half as I pull my hand away.

"I've seen them, I mean." I curl my hand into a fist. "I don't want you to think I'm weird." Glancing away, I stare at the fire for a moment. "I did grow up in a community of primarily humans, though." Memories flicker through my mind, making me lose myself for a breath until Lawson's hand touches my knee.

"It's okay, love." His voice is gentle as he touches my chin, tapping it with his index finger. "Don't focus on any of that. Focus on getting some rest tonight. We'll handle the weather tomorrow. You're safe here."

I *feel* safe as Boone and Reid come back with all the blankets and pillows from the room I saw, plus more. They take the time to arrange them all around the couch, and Reid takes the far end, stretching his long body out on a chaise that looks special-made to encompass him. Boone hands me a pillow, then a blanket, then shuffles around to hand me *another* pillow.

"You should sleep in the middle since it's closer to the fire." He looks down at me from behind the couch. "None of us will freeze, but you might."

I frown at him. "Are you discriminating against me because I'm a human?"

"No." Boone pauses, throwing a pillow at Lawson's head. "I'm merely pointing out that you have terrible survival skills, little miss." He grins as I lift one of the pillows threateningly.

"Don't," Reid drawls from the end of the couch. "If Lawson's horns ruin these pillows, we'll have nothing to sleep on."

I lower my arm like a scolded child, shifting up the couch until I'm closer to Reid. He turns his head to look at me, before opening an arm. My stomach swoops as I lay my pillows down and then curl up against his side. His fur radiates heat as I curl up under a blanket too, sighing softly as I watch Boone and Lawson adjust themselves.

Boone helps Lawson lie down so his horns don't get in the way of anyone, then settles himself down near him, pressing a kiss to Lawson's long nose. Lawson smiles, then tilts his head to kiss Boone back gently, leaving it chaste as they wind their fingers together.

Reid pulls me close with his arm. As my body rolls into his, my head moves slightly off the pillows, landing partially on his chest. Two thumps echo out of his breastbone and I look down at him in surprise. He tucks the blanket closer before saying, "two hearts" like it's more than enough explanation.

"It's what makes him love both of us," Boone jokes from the other end of the couch. "Just be thankful he's not green and smells like onions —" Lawson smacks him with a pillow to get him to shut up as I laugh against Reid's chest.

Reid says nothing as he pushes my hair away from my face, tipping his head down to look at me with a slightly soft expression. "I'm glad we found you, Lily." My heart flips as his gentle fingers tuck my hair behind an ear. "You should sleep though, snowflake. Hopefully the power will be back by morning."

I swallow, nodding as I readjust so I'm comfortable curled up against him. It doesn't feel weird, just incomplete with Boone and Lawson farther away, and I wonder for a moment if I've pushed them away from sleeping next to their partner. They don't seem to mind, back to exchanging soft words at the other end of the couch. My eyes slip closed, tired but thinking too much as I adjust again.

Reid doesn't stir as I try to settle. When I move to fully lay my head on his chest, I wrap an arm around him loosely, sinking into the warmth coming off him. He finally lays a hand on my back, rubbing it slowly as he sighs.

I lie there with my eyes closed as his chest moves steadily up and down, willing myself to fall asleep, or at least relax enough that I know it'll come eventually, but I *can't*. Flashes of the day assault me, from slipping down the ridge to the feeling of Reid picking me up and carrying me all the way to the cabin, to Lawson catching me and getting me out of my soaked clothes, to Boone sitting in the literal shower to warm me up.

They all dropped everything to help me.

I try to keep my breathing even as I remember the way Boone cupped my sore throat. It should have scared me shitless, but instead I fight the urge to press my legs together even now, cognizant of all three of them in the room.

The fire crackles, spitting little embers into the air as my hand moves absent-mindedly on Reid's torso. His curls slip through my fingers, tight to his chest. He breathes into the touch as my hand drags up and down. He watched Boone and me in the shower — he saw me partially naked.

And Lawson was ready to dress me after the shower.

I still my hand, scared that I'm crossing a line. Reid stays quiet as I tilt my head up, watching his face in the dim light. His eyes are closed, but his jaw looks a little tight. Moving slowly, I press my lips together as I cast a look behind me at Boone and Lawson.

I'm either about to end up in the snow outside, or have the best night of my life.

Freezing is apparently still a risk I'm willing to take as I glide my hand down Reid's chest, running it over his fur-covered abs. His eyes open slowly, staring down at me as I pause just above the waistband of his shorts.

We stare at each other, a thousand questions unspoken as I hesitate, then whisper, "I want to thank you."

His eyelids droop as he inclines his chin at me. "It's not necessary. I want to make that crystal clear. We will sleep in another room and leave you alone." I can feel the heat of two more eyes on us the moment Reid speaks.

I dip my hand under his waistband. The fur feels coarse against my fingers as I find the length of him, thick in my hand. Wrapping my fingers around him, I jerk my hand up, then down, watching his face as he drops his head back to the couch with a loud groan.

There's not a chance in hell that Boone can't smell my arousal, just like in the bathroom. Leaning up, I let Reid go as I pull at his pants, managing to get them down over his thighs, revealing him to me. His cock is *huge*, big enough my fingers don't meet when I wrap my hand around him. The only difference to a human is the light dusting of fur near the base, leaving the head, shaft, and tip exposed, save for his foreskin, which rolls over him when my hand moves. His throat bobs as I pull my hand away and then lick my palm, returning to stroke him slowly.

Bending over on the couch, I pull his foreskin back, then suck the tip into my mouth, moaning softly. His hips jolt just slightly at the feeling, and it's enough to make me smile as I try to take him deeper. There's no way to do it, so I settle on slurping and licking at his head, covering him in spit as my hand does most of the work, using the other to brace myself against his thighs.

The noise of me sucking Reid's cock is only occasionally cut by the sound of the fire popping. Even though I know Lawson and Boone have to be watching, I don't stop. It makes me hotter, warmer, drinking up the idea that they're watching their partner be rewarded for saving my life.

Moaning around the stretch of Reid in my mouth, I lift up again and then spit directly on his dick.

"Holy fuck," Boone breathes out as I fist Reid's tip to smear my spit.

Twisting my hand, I slide it up and down a few times, keeping my grip tight as Reid grunts softly, nodding his head. "Like that. Fist me harder and jerk me, snowflake. Do it right."

Shivering, I focus on stimulating his head, reaching down to lightly tease his balls, which are also fuzzy, though less so than the rest of him. He lets out a full-throated moan as I knead him with one hand and then let him fuck himself against my fist with the other. After a moment, I shake my head, letting him go as I gasp, "I can make this even better."

The sweatshirt comes off in an instant, then the shirt, leaving me in just a pair of someone's boxers and socks. My breasts hang, full and low as I straddle Reid's thick thighs. He stares down at me, his lips parting as I press my chest together and then spit between them, lubing them up before pressing his cock between them.

Reid curses, his hips pumping up experimentally. "*Christ.*"

I'd need some prep before I tried to take him, but I still want to try. This works for now as I lean down to lick his head when he thrusts up far enough. He lets out another muttered string of profanity as I suck on his tip, moaning and letting him move a little faster. With each thrust through my breasts, I leave my mouth open so he can enter it at the end. Holding my breasts together makes my shoulders hurt a little, but when Reid speeds up slightly, I look up at him under my lashes as he pulls back before thrusting, smearing pre-cum across my parted lips.

It tastes like spiced berries and I lick my lips with a moan, staring at him as he starts to pound up faster. Reid reaches down, helping me squeeze my boobs together tighter, nodding as he moans and focuses on getting off. "That's good. That's *really* good, snowflake. Are you going to let me come all over your tits?"

I nod rapidly, sucking on his leaking tip before he pulls it away again. With a gasp, I chase it, bending my neck as I keep my mouth open. "My face too if you want."

There's a moan from the other end of the couch, and I wish desperately my throat wasn't sore and that I could take Reid immediately as my clit throbs. It doesn't matter because he reaches one hand to brace it on my head, pushing me down as his cock starts to thrust hard and fast between my boobs. "Spit on it."

I spit, watching as it smears with his next thrust, then take him deeper when the tip slides past my lips. Choking slightly, I hold him in place as I swallow around him, feeling his thighs shake as he pushes my head down. It's all I can do to breathe through my nose as my eyes sting, tears threatening to overflow before he comes with a roar that rattles the windows.

The amount of cum that spurts out of him makes me gasp. I swallow some, but the rest splashes out of my mouth as he slips free. It gets on my face, then across my chest in thick puddles as he sinks back to the couch, breathing hard with a hand still on my head.

I lean back, flushed and needy as I press my thighs together and turn to look at Boone and Lawson. They're upright now, both sitting on the couch. Boone's hand is in Lawson's lap, while Lawson fists Boone, jerking him just out of his boxers.

I go to Boone first since he's closer, kneeling between his legs to look up at him. His chest moves slowly as Lawson's hand slips away, revealing a thick bulb at the base of his short cock. His tip twitches as I reach for him, able to wrap my fingers around him as I replicate what Lawson was doing. Boone stares at me, his voice husky. "It's a stopper, meant to keep the cum in, just like Lawson's knot. Reid can take it, Lawson can't."

Kneeling up, I suck him down my throat, moaning around him before pulling back when my lips kiss the bulb. "It's big."

Boone nods, laser-focused on me as I suck him off, using a hand to squeeze and rub the mass of swollen muscle at the base of him. His balls jerk slightly each time I massage it, and I lick a little stream of cum that leaks out, savoring it as I bob my head. It's easier to suck him off when he actually fits in my mouth, and Boone grabs a handful of my hair, holding it for me as I clench my thighs together.

He grunts, tugging at my hair with the same pace of his hips when they start to thrust up into my mouth. "That's it. Let me fill that warm little mouth with cum. Then I'll let Lawson have you all used and messed up."

My clit throbs as I moan, nodding my head as his bulb keeps smacking against my mouth. Spreading my lips wider, I fight to take it. It's clear that I can't, so I squeeze it harder, digging my nails into it experimentally.

Boone comes off the couch with a loud groan, then his whole body twitches. When he comes, I manage to swallow more than Reid. Laying Boone's tip on my tongue, I open my mouth and look up at him, allowing him to watch as he spurts straight onto my tongue. His eyes widen, his lips parting as he flops back to the couch.

Lawson's hands are on me before I can shift to kneel in front of him. Instead, he lifts me from the floor and pulls me against his chest, breathing hard. "I want to kiss you, love. Is that an option?"

My stomach curls with pleasure as I nod. I'm a wreck on top of him, sticky with remnants of Reid's cum and my mouth red from Boone's cock. It doesn't stop Lawson as he pulls me into a kiss. It's only awkward for a moment as I find my way, kissing across his lips to encompass his snout, feeling the thickness of him through his pants as he widens my thighs and grinds me down on top of him.

I moan softly, cupping his face as I roll into the movement.

Lawson's fingers hook into the waistband of my borrowed boxers, then tug them down over my hips. When they're finally off, I stay partially lifted, kissing him as he fights to shed his own clothes. The moment his pants are down, his cock flops up on his abdomen. He's thick, somewhere between Boone and Reid, with a tell-tale knot at the base, smaller than Boone's and something I can definitely take.

Breathing hard, I stare at his length. "I want to fuck you."

"Thank god," he grunts, pulling me into another kiss as he rubs against me. His thick cock is easy to grind against, smearing my arousal and the pre-cum absolutely dribbling from him. It eases the slide of us against each other as he braces his hands on my hips.

"Now?"

"Now," I moan, reaching down to grab him and push his broad head into me. Just the tip teases in and out as I rock down, adjusting to his size. Pressing a kiss to the side of his mouth, I pant against his soft fur, grasping at the couch behind his head when I roll my hips up, then down, taking a little more.

As his length pushes in, it becomes easier to just grab onto the base of his horns. Lawson moans when my fingers scrape the place where they meet his skull. Then hands touch me from behind and I arch back, my head moving to stare as Reid pushes me down onto Lawson. My lips part in a surprised gasp, taking more and more until Lawson is twitching inside of me, his hooves scrambling on the wooden floors.

Boone reaches out, his hand grasping one of my breasts and rolling a nipple between two fingers. Lawson captures my mouth with another kiss before he pulls out slightly and thrusts back up into me. I ride him, holding onto his horns as Reid's hands push down on my shoulders, forcing his knot to kiss my cunt with each thrust. Boone focuses on my breasts, leaning between my chest and Lawson's to suck at them, twisting my nipples and tugging until they're red and I'm breathing heavily.

The overstimulation is almost too much, too fast. Lawson's thrusts become ragged, making my body jiggle with the impact as Reid pushes me harder down on him each time. His knot threatens to stretch me once, then pulls back, leaving me spasming at the loss. Lawson curses, holding onto the back of my neck as he breathes against my lips.

"If I knot you, I can make sure I get out. Is that okay? We don't have to wait for it to deflate. I can keep fucking you."

I shiver, the words all I need as I slam my hips back down into his. He lets out a low moan, huffing as I take him almost completely on the first try. The knot pops back out when I rise up, and then on the next one, Reid holds me in place as Lawson's hips smack up into mine. This time he enters me fully, making us both tremble as I clench and then shake around him. The pressure is *intense* as my head spins. Boone sucks on my right breast, nipping at me as his other hand raises, holding the front of my throat as Lawson braces the back.

I come with a silent scream, no noise coming out as I convulse around Lawson, leaning against Reid as my entire body trembles. Every muscle in my body shudders from the exertion as Lawson rocks up into me, then floods me with his own orgasm. My thighs burn as I catch my breath. My eyes open in time to see his hand move between us, barely grazing my clit enough to make me flutter. When my muscles spasm, he slips a finger between my walls and himself, pushing his knot down and releasing himself from me.

The pressure leaves me, along with a puddle of his cum, landing in his lap. My heart pounds in my ears as I lick my lips. "I want more."

Reid chuckles behind me, then clicks his tongue. "Boone, up. Fuck me while I stretch her even wider."

Boone pulls away from my chest, but not before moving his head up and capturing my lips in a deep kiss. My toes curl as I reach out for him, my mind spinning at the way his kiss is so firm — like it's a finite seal of approval to what just happened. Then he's gone, moving up to brace a leg on the couch while Reid adjusts himself to kneel.

Lawson lies down while holding me. I turn over, putting my back to his chest as Reid settles between my thighs, sandwiching me between him and Lawson. Boone looms behind Reid, stroking himself and twisting his bulb as he sucks on a thumb, then presses it between Reid's asscheeks. Reid's eyelids flutter before he bends over me and runs his hands up and down my thighs, smearing Lawson's cum. Sliding two fingers into me, he spreads them, then nods and pulls them out, pressing the tip of himself into me.

"You won't be able to take all of it. I'm too long."

I stare at him as his foreskin slips back, exposing his head as he pushes into me, thrusting in and out with just the first couple inches. The pressure and pleasure of being so full immediately after my orgasm makes me melt back into Lawson, breathing in with each thrust, and out when Reid slides away.

Boone forces Reid to bend slightly, then guides himself to Reid's ass. He pushes in without warning, making Reid stutter and thrust deeper accidentally. My toes curl as I grasp at Reid's forearm with one hand and Lawson's with another. I can feel Lawson hardening under my ass as the motion of Boone fucking into Reid carries over to Reid fucking me. Each thrust sends a ricochet of moans through the room as I rub against Lawson.

It takes no time at all before Boone curses and presses

deeper. Reid grunts, bending down to kiss me just as Boone lets out a loud snarl, signaling his bulb is fully seated. It pushes Reid deeper into me, thick enough that I swear I feel him in my throat as he begins to steadily fuck me. Lawson's leaking cock under me smears across my ass before slipping between my cheeks. He uses it like Reid used my chest, humping up into me from behind with the motion of Reid.

Crying out, I clench around Reid as his fangs catch my lower lip. A flash of pain echoes from my mouth, and I know without a doubt that he nicked me with one of them as he shakes above us, pounding deeper on his next thrust only to come with a broken groan. His orgasm sets Boone off again, then Lawson. I lie there, stuffed full and struggling as I writhe against Reid, gasping, "P-please finish me."

He lifts his head, his eyes flashing dark as Lawson reaches up to grasp my throat with a hand. Boone reaches between Reid and I, rubbing my clit rapidly as Reid pulls back and fucks his cum into me. I stare up, feeling the flush spread as I start to shake, the orgasm bringing me to an edge with no end in sight as all my nerve endings short-circuit like the faulty wiring in the cabin.

My climax hits just as Reid pulls out and I feel his tip slip free from the power of my muscles convulsing down. My breathing saws in and out as Lawson holds onto my throat, only applying slight pressure, but it's enough to leave me completely spent on top of him, dripping everywhere.

Reid looks down at us as Boone pulls out. Reid cups my face softly, then smiles. "I'll get something to clean us up." He turns, kissing Boone softly before leaving the room. Lawson's cum smears across my back as we both shift. I push up on shaking arms, watching as Boone sits down and wraps another hand around himself. He jerks himself again, eyes flickering between me and Lawson. Lawson shifts me carefully to place me on the couch, before getting up to sit beside Boone.

Reid returns with the washcloths just as Lawson reaches to help Boone. I watch as Reid abandons the washcloths near me, then strides over, taking control of the situation by sitting down and dragging Boone into his lap. Boone straddles Reid just like I did to Lawson when I took his knot, but this time, it gives Reid the perfect vantage to fist his own cock with Boone's, his hand large enough to encompass them both. Boone's shoulders tremble as Reid jerks his hand hard and fast, so rough that it makes my skin prickle, wishing I was like them, wishing I could *take* that from both of them.

Boone's forehead meets Reid's as he starts to breathe heavier. Lawson reaches between them, carefully squeezing Boone's bulb, before digging his nails into it. Boone comes again just as he and Reid kiss, spurt after spurt landing on Reid's chest, combining with Reid's orgasm, which is smaller. They breathe hard, then turn to look at me.

With a smirk, Boone finally relaxes. "That was a good time, little miss."

I flush, crawling across the couch to the three of them. I don't know who kisses me first — Boone or Reid — because as soon as someone grabs me, another pair of hands replaces him. Someone snatches up a washcloth, wiping me between my thighs and making me twitch back into them. The last mouth I taste is Lawson as I tug him down by the horns and smile.

Reid throws a blanket over all of us as we pile into a mess of limbs where there's not a wet spot. It only lasts for five minutes until Reid stands with a grumble, picking me up first and smacking my hip. I yelp sleepily, slung over his shoulder as he grabs multiple pillows. Boone and Lawson follow us to the dark bedroom. My heart jolts a little, until hands touch me, gently pulling me down to a big bed. Soft fur lands against my cheek, a nose presses against my back, and I tangle up with all of them in the plush bed, too spent to think about the logistics of what may happen when morning comes.

When the sun does rise, the power comes back on. This time the news announces that it'll take at least four days for the snow to clear naturally.

I take it for the sign it is. To stay. To be with them.

And then I fall back into bed with a minotaur, a yeti, and bear shifter without a care in the world.

ASSISTANCE NEEDED

Personal Assistant Needed: Full-time, on-call hours, contact below.

The office building is far grander than I imagined from the scant job description. It looms overhead with stonework ledges for gargoyle guards to perch above the two-story entrance consisting of — what appears to be — glass doors with solid gold inlays.

In a word, it's *fancy*.

A doorman lets me in after I tell him my name, directing me to walk to the large front desk where a security guard is stationed next to a receptionist. The guard, a naga, flicks his rattling tail back and forth idly, not irate, just bored as he scans my ID to confirm who I am, then releases me to talk to the receptionist.

He's the nicest person so far, smiling up at me as his green fairy wings flutter behind him. When I sign in, he stands to walk me to the elevators, leaning in partially to key in a number on the pad next to the elevator panel. "The boss *never* brings someone upstairs." The fairy smiles at me. "Good luck, but I think you've got it."

My chest warms at his words. As the elevator doors close, I suck in a slow breath, letting it out after waiting a few seconds. This will be okay. I will get this job. Admittedly, I was desperate when I replied to the listing, only visible in the back of the Sunday paper — but everything I've tried since moving here has gone... honestly? Pretty fucking terribly.

There was the fact that the apartment I chose to rent sight-unseen actually has an awful roach problem. Then my roommate bailed, citing that she actually decided to take a summer in Europe. I do *not* have 'summer in Europe' money. Then the job I *moved* to the city for was suddenly not mine, because the Editor-in-Chief's nephew decided he wanted experience working at a magazine.

I've scraped together my measly savings, using it as sparingly as humanly possible to not only keep a roof over my head, but also eat at least once a day. I've even pet-sat for the people in the apartment blocks around me, trying to make extra cash where I can by walking dogs while others are at work, feeding fish when they're gone for a long weekend, and even watching a snake... do snake things for a few days while my neighbor was gone. There's a food bank not far from my place at a huge Catholic church, where — thankfully — they give out free sandwiches a few times a week. I've eaten *so much* peanut butter.

Still, I'm in my best today. Albeit, my dress hangs off my shoulders, looser than before. I still fill it out enough to feel polished, eyeing myself carefully in the mirrored walls. With my hair pulled back, it hides some of the natural grays already growing in at the crown, interspersed in the rest of the chestnut strands. If nothing else, my resume was good enough to get in here, and that means I can find another job if this doesn't pan out.

I really hope it pans out. I need a win for once.

Fidgeting, I swallow as the elevator jolts. The display above the doors flies past ten floors at a time, rising and rising until I'm aloft near level one hundred. It begins to slow, ticking up twenty more levels, before stopping. The doors ding as they open to a wide entryway, a single desk at the front.

It's empty.

I step out of the elevator slowly, looking around at the polished walls and ceiling. There's nothing, save for the desk, so I step around it, looking to see if I missed something. It's so bare there's a layer of dust finely coating it. It's not filthy by any stretch of the imagination, but unused. I guess they do need an assistant.

Turning to the side, I peer down a short hall, staring at a pair of doors open where light casually streams out. My heels click on the tile floor as I make my way down the hall, praying I'm making the right choice as I step into the other space.

One entire wall is glass, floor to ceiling. Staring down at the city from this vantage point makes me a bit dizzy, because nothing looks real. There are still floors above, but the elevator must only go to them with another code. This room has a couple couches, then a larger oak desk angled toward the door.

From an adjoining room, footsteps sound. I straighten immediately, nothing in my hands as I stand near the entrance. The man that enters is tall, with jet black hair and fine, sharp features. His brow is angled, giving him a permanent scowl — but it's the *horns* coming out of his head that make my breath stop.

They're winding and as black as his hair, shimmering onyx in the light as they twist away from his head like spires, curling around on themselves and stretching toward the tall ceilings.

Heavy, *thick* wings hang off his back, almost dragging the ground. The leather rustles on them as the man turns and takes note of me with a slight inclination of his head. He's intimidating, but he also looks completely exhausted.

"Please sit." He motions to one of the couches. "This will be an informal interview."

My mouth goes dry as I nod, stepping down where the couches are slightly recessed into the floor. Perching on a cushion, I follow him with my eyes as he walks to a small cabinet and pours something that looks like liquid gold into a glass goblet. He lifts it to his lips and takes a drink, then walks over, placing it on a side table before taking a seat on the other couch.

"You responded to the personal assistant advertisement." I can't place his accent, something vaguely Eastern European. When I nod again, he raises an eyebrow at me. "You can speak, can't you?"

"Yes," I fumble out, forcing my hands to stay still in my lap. "I apologize. I just..." My eyes dart around the room, watching a literal cloud float past the windows. "I assumed I would have a meeting with your HR department first, to see if we're a fit."

"I can ascertain that, thank you." His voice drops to a rumble as he picks up the glass again to drink. "This is not a normal assistant position. You would not be paid through any of my companies, you would be privately employed for me alone."

I blink at him. "Mister..."

"Call me Reyes." His eyes flick to me, golden flecks swimming in the pure black of them. They resemble a lizard, except they're inverted. The slash through the center is a startling gold, the only bright spot in the colorless void. When he blinks, a third lid closes over them briefly, before retracting.

"Mister Reyes," I try again, slightly moving on the couch

to stare at him. "I am committed, of course, to being your full-time personal assistant, but what tasks would I be handling?"

He takes another drink, his throat moving. Scales flutter up his skin, just as dark as his horns, rippling like he's fighting a full shift. It hits me, all of the sudden, that if he fully shifted he'd blow the top off this building — because he isn't a demon, or another shifter — he's a *dragon.*

Reyes breathes out, smoke exhaling from his lips as he places the empty goblet on the table. The scales ripple away again as he looks at me.

"I need assistance."

When he doesn't say anything more, I balk at him. "Personal tasks? Schedule planning? A note-taker?" All things I can do — but the lack of information is really making my skin crawl.

Reyes shrugs. "All, eventually." He turns to look at the windows and I watch his shoulders as they flex. His wings rustle as he stands again, letting them flare out and stretch. They're so long that they nearly brush a wall before he lets them fold again. The leather compresses, and I tilt my head up to stare as one of his hands fidgets, fisting, then relaxing.

"Alright," I find myself saying, palms in my lap. "You need someone every hour of the day to take care of every task that crops up. Let's discuss pay."

He looks down at me suddenly, his forehead creasing. "You would live here. I would supply everything."

Even though I should be flinching away from the red flags, I can't help but let my eyes wander around the room. "Here?"

Reyes shakes his head, nodding above us. "My personal apartments are on the upper two floors. You would stay there until I need you."

Tilting my chin up, I stare at the ceiling like I'll be able to see through the layers of steel beams and tile. "I'm failing to understand what exactly this position is, Mister Reyes."

He picks up the glass goblet, twisting it between two fingers before wiping some of the gold residue off the rim. It bubbles on his finger, then begins to drip down his hand. He simply replaces the goblet on the table, then uses his other hand to push the gold back up, gathering it until he can compress it into a small disc. It shimmers orange and red until he breathes smoke onto it, forcing it to cool. Carefully, he places it on the couch next to me.

"That is pure, from my hoard. I will be returning there shortly to sleep. Dragons sleep for long periods of time. It's inevitable that it would come, though sad it had to happen now." He looks back at the windows. "I will need someone trustworthy to run my companies in my stead."

The full effect of what he's asking hits me. I stare at the gold disc, afraid to touch it as I whisper, "And you... want to hire me to do that?"

"I liked your resume, Maisie." It's the first time he utters my name. Reyes looks back at me, blinking slowly again. "I grow very tired these days. Would you be able to step into my roles by the end of the week? I will sleep for six months, then return."

My heart jumps in my chest as I nod slowly. "Six months."

"Yes." He yawns, then turns away from me, his wings dragging behind him as he walks toward the other door. "Please talk to Faenir on the ground floor about coordinating your access codes and moving what you wish upstairs. Take the gold."

My hand stretches, palm covering the disc as I watch him leave the room.

I still feel like I didn't do anything to earn this lofty position as I find my way back to the elevator and ride it down.

Faenir, the fairy, greets me with a large smile. "Reyes already sent over your information. Would you like me to coordinate a moving van for you?"

I think about the few boxes I have left in my apartment, then shake my head. "No, I can move it here."

He offers me a smaller smile, then slides multiple cards across the desk to me. "This will be your access to the upper levels. Hold it against the elevator panel and it will reveal the buttons." Tapping a black metal card with a sharp nail, Faenir's lips twitch. "This is Reyes's personal card. You have no limits. Make the spaces feel like your own in his absence. I'll coordinate the first few meetings to let the boards know you'll be acting in his stead during his slumber."

I nod dumbly, taking whatever he gives me before stepping back out onto the street. In the span of a ten-minute conversation I went from desperately hoping for a job offer to holding the keys to a company. I can barely comprehend it — though I *know* my resume speaks for itself. I know my worth, and I refuse to question that, even if the circumstances seem strange at the moment. I don't know anything about dragon culture, or this sleep he seems primed to take. Who am I to question what Reyes wants to do with his own businesses?

The metal card feels heavy in my hand when I clutch it tighter and turn on a dime, striding toward the nearest restaurant. It seems like the right choice to start with taking care of myself.

He entrusted this all to me. I'm going to make sure he doesn't regret it.

I only saw Reyes three times in the two weeks while I settled in. Then he disappeared somewhere outside of the city. Faenir gave me the address in a packet of information about all of the companies Reyes either has a stake in, or founded himself. By my estimation after studying the paperwork, he's close to a millennia old, give or take a few centuries. Some of the companies are in antiquities, which feels very fitting for a dragon, while others are charitable.

Then there are the ones that make him money. Lots of it.

The black card *doesn't* have a limit. Faenir just blinked at me the day I suggested that I'd like to buy a few items for the room I picked on the upper floors, like I was dumb for seeking *his* approval. The apartment is double-height, with off shooting spaces to encompass a private office I work out of often, and then the bedroom I chose. It's tucked at the back of the building, with a wall that overlooks the water and the bay. It's pleasant at night to stare out at the dark sky, knowing that past the pollution of the city there are thousands of twinkling stars.

Needless to say, I'm making a few changes while Reyes is gone.

"Hello Paul!" Striding through the main doors, I pass by the small sitting area outfitted in the bottom of the building now. There are three plush couches and a variety of chairs. In the other empty area, I hired out a local orc's coffee shop to have a small pop-up. If it keeps being as popular as it has been, I plan on installing a proper coffee bar and making them a permanent part of the building.

The naga security guard raises a hand, smiling at me as I stride to his desk and slide a doughnut box across the surface to him. "Cream filled with sprinkles." Turning to Faenir, I give him three portfolios first, bending over the desk. "Did you find your replacement yet?"

He scoffs at me. "I'm not moving from this desk. I *love* reception."

Pouting at him, I nudge a fairy-cake from the coffee cart toward him. "But..."

He snatches it up with a little toothy grin. "Your bribes don't work on me, but I *will* still reap the benefits of taking them."

Rolling my eyes, I flip open the top portfolio, going over where I need it delivered. The first twenty floors are all of the staff encompassing the charitable arm of Reyes's empire, and I like funneling as much money as I can in that direction since he has it coming from so many avenues. I've already found plans for an interspecies orphanage that he was in the beginning stages of — which is now close to being restored after I bought an abandoned school facility just outside of the city. Part of the dorms are being converted, while the main classrooms will be used for the kids' education and night classes for the local community.

Faenir takes the portfolios. "You work too much."

I scoff at him, but Paul takes a huge bite of a doughnut, his jaw unhinging as he shoves the rest in. "You do."

Shaking my head at them both, I fidget, glancing down at the disc hanging around my neck. I had a witch add a small hole to the gold, providing an unbreakable chain so I can wear it constantly without fear. It's a reminder of how much is at stake and how much I've been left in charge of. Fiddling with it, I let out a breath. "Just doing my job."

"Go take a break. He was never this involved." Faenir waves me off. "Go to your tower, Maisie, some of us have calls to make."

I take the dismissal for what it is, walking empty-handed to the elevators. There's actually a private one off to the side that I use now. It's just me as I ride up one hundred floors, then slow to a stop at the apartment. Stepping out, I kick my heels off into a little pile, padding across the wood floor while pulling my hair up into a bun on my head. It's always just me, and this high up, it feels like I'm the only person in the world sometimes.

A pang of loneliness hits as I turn one of the huge TVs on, flipping over to the stock market to keep an eye on Reyes's investments as I scrounge through the kitchen. One of the other decisions I made for myself was hiring a *very* talented private chef, who leaves me prepared meals three times a week, and sometimes comes over to cook. I like those nights, it means I have someone to talk to.

The middle section of floors below me house people working all hours, but it's not like I can just drop in. That would be almost as bizarre as the random marketing firm on floor fifty-seven. I've still not figured out why Reyes funded it — but that's above me. When I'm bored, which is often enough, I read through all the paperwork in his office, figuring out what I can. Most of it is organized, and some even have notes, but they're old and written by someone named Baoriec. I tried to search the name in the internal records system, but nothing came up.

I can only assume they were the one that came before me.

Tugging a container of chicken and rice from the fridge, I pop it onto a plate and then stick it in the microwave, holding my phone in one hand as I idly scroll. It's very... weird. Sometimes it hits me that I've been here for months, stepping into the role Reyes played. He treated a lot of the companies like self-running factories, but a lot of them actually *did* need someone to pay attention. Some of the fixes were as easy as allocating funds so the businesses didn't have to feel strapped for supplies, or had extra cash for catered lunches.

The microwave beeps and I pull my dinner out, stabbing a bite of chicken with my fork as I stare at my phone. After a few minutes, I leave it on the counter and focus on eating. Just as I bend to put my plate in the dishwasher, my phone buzzes three times in rapid succession.

Faenir's name pops up. I slide to answer immediately, toggling him to speaker phone.

"I've cleared your meetings for the next week."

"Excuse me?" I nearly drop my fork on my foot as I turn to give my phone a sharp look.

"You need to go to the manor. He'll want you there when he wakes up."

Reaching for my phone, I flip to the calendar, counting back the weeks until I come to the day I interviewed. Five months and two weeks ago. Staring at the screen, I nod my head. "I'll pack a bag."

"One of the cars will be waiting." Faenir hangs up.

My pulse jumps as I turn the TV off, making sure everything is alright as I drift down the hall to my room. I painted the walls that aren't windows a light shade of yellow, and in the waning light they look ablaze. Finding a suitcase in the huge closet, I fill it slowly, packing a mixture of business attire and casual options. The packet went over this. As it gets closer to him waking up, I need to be there to support him — but it hurts a little to know everything that I've spent almost half a year building up will be taken away from me when he's back.

But that's what I agreed to.

I clasp the suitcase, changing into an athleisure set before shrugging on a half-zip. When I get to the ground floor again, most of the day workers have gone, leaving the lobby empty with the coffee cart closed for the day. The car meets me outside, and a nice human who's driven me around before greets me as I climb into the back.

"Settle in, miss. It'll be almost three hours before we get to the estate."

I open a book on my phone, but end up with my head

leaned back against the carseat, drifting in and out of consciousness as the movement of the car lulls me into a fitful sleep. My mind is too preoccupied with what I may find when I get to the house. I know it's huge and that it's been with Reyes since he moved to America. It has to be large enough to encompass a dragon, and I don't know exactly how large he is fully shifted.

The sky darkens as we're driving through rural areas, winding up northern roads. The car makes a turn and a large golden gate opens for us automatically. It takes another almost thirty minutes to get from the road to the house that rises up on the top of a hill. Even in the dark I can see the intricate stone and brickwork, the walls almost endlessly expanding to either side.

"Faenir wanted me to tell you that there will be a food delivery tomorrow morning." The driver helps me out, grabbing my bag for me. I take it and let myself in, watching the car leave as I enter the stagnant house.

It takes me a few tries to find the lights. When they flicker on, I take in the gilded frames spanning the entry hall. They're all portraits of Reyes — but throughout the centuries. The oldest is the largest, with a painted portrait of his bust looking off to the left, a pattern of black scales behind him. My heart jumps as I walk through the empty house, then travel up the stairs after finding out the main floor is just a multiple living areas, two huge kitchens, and a library.

Upstairs is full of doors, offshoots leading to random rooms. I pick one, stepping into a suite with a huge bed and sitting area near a fire. Leaving my bag by a chest of drawers, I fish my phone out and open the digital copy of the paperwork Faenir gave me months ago.

At the very end pages, there are a few notes.

When you arrive at his estate, he will sense you. The entrance to his chambers is hidden behind the main stairwell. Descend down to find his hoard. Everything from there is up to your discretion.

I pull my jacket closer and turn around, making my way back down the stairs to poke around the rooms. Finally, I find a wall that is partially crooked, and when I press my hand against it, it pops open, releasing an exhale like the house can breathe on its own.

The *heat* coming from the revealed stairs blows my hair back. I leave the passage open behind me as I walk down the stone steps carefully, twisting my way until I begin to see little shimmers of light flickering off of the walls like firelight. When I round the last bend, it opens up to a huge room, a hollowing of the very hill the house sits atop.

Mountains of gold greet me. Coins, shields, treasure chests, and more sparkle under blue and green dragon fire lights, burning eternally as long as the dragon is alive. And he *is*.

Reyes sleeps in the center of the pile of gemstones and precious metals. His dragon could overtake a football field or soccer pitch easily. Smoke leaves his wide nostrils in little puffs as he breathes in and out. His onyx scales shimmer under the flickering flames, glimmering as much as the gems underneath him as his tail twitches. The tip of it is feathered, along with the ridges on his spine, an unexpected juxtaposition to the hardness of his scales. His ears fidget on his head, his horns much the same as the way they are in his human form, only larger and deadlier.

Stretching one muscled arm out, Reyes's claws send a pile scattering. I reach up and rub the disc around my throat impulsively as I take a deep breath. He doesn't stir again, but his head does move slightly to face me, like he can sense me.

"Hi," I whisper, pressing the disc between two fingers. "I've done a lot while you've rested. I even started the orphanage plans. It'll be done by the time you wake up, and we can go over the launch." I don't know why I talk, but it feels right as I sink to sit on a pile of treasure. It's softer than it appears, slipping under me as I fold my legs and rest my chin on my knees. "I didn't change much in the apartment, though I did paint my room. Thank you for leaving me the card." It's easier to talk to him this way, and I'm convinced he can't hear me because his chest remains steadily rising and falling with each breath.

"I'm going to sleep upstairs in the first room I found." I twist the disc on my throat. "The packet didn't say that you needed me to keep an eye on you. But I'm here and will be when you do finally wake up."

When there's no response, I stand again, brushing my leggings off with my hands and turning. There's a soft exhalation of more smoke, and it curls around me as I climb the stairs, leaving the door partially cracked.

The grocery delivery does come the next day. A green witch arrives with a minotaur in tow. The two of them stock one of the kitchens, chatting happily with me. As the witch leaves, she waves excitedly. "I'm so glad he has someone here when he wakes up this time!" The statement leaves me confused as I give her a polite smile, closing the door.

The library is so huge that it takes me a solid three hours to find my first mention of Baoriec, stashed as notes in the margins of a classic book. The description is of a lover in an old poetry collection, with a scrawled note next to a couplet that reads: '*fair as summer sun / meant to be the one*'.

Reyes has underlined *the one* and drawn a line to Baoriec's name.

My heart clenches as I slip the book back in its place. I check on Reyes briefly that night, lingering near the stairs as I watch him sleep. It feels wrong to speak again, so I leave him to climb upstairs. The room I chose has a huge attached bathroom, with a dragon clawfoot tub that I fill with steaming hot water. It stings my skin when I sink into the bath, sighing and resting my head against the ceramic side.

The bubbles I found stashed under the cabinet smell like cinnamon and I sink lower, swirling my hand through them. Stretching a leg out, I embrace the heat on my tired muscles, my hair swept off my neck into a messy tumble at the top of my head. In the silence, I can only hear the water sloshing as I ease a hand underwater and move it between my thighs, cupping myself.

I've been working for months, my only company being the few people that I pay from Reyes's money. I can't remember the last person I slept with — but it has to have been before I moved to the city.

My fingers slip lower, parting myself and gliding over my clit. Moaning softly, I press my cheek against the cool ceramic, circling the bundle of nerves with slow strokes. The water sluices against my skin, the scent of cinnamon burning my senses as I inhale and rub tight little circles. The flush in my veins feels twice as intense in the warm water as I breathe out against the side of the tub, my muscles fluttering between my thighs. I leave my clit and angle my hand, thrusting a finger into myself. It's not a good position, because it feels too shallow.

Leaning up in the water, I stand suddenly, grabbing my towel for the barest of moments before going into the room and tearing through my suitcase. I find a glass dildo with multiple ridges running down it, then return to the tub, sliding back into the warm water's embrace before resting a foot on the edge.

I push the dildo into me with a choked moan, adjusting to the feeling of the thick tip filling me. After a moment, I push it deeper, feeling the second ridge settle. With little rocking motions, I fuck myself, throwing my head back as the water sloshes up the edges of the tub. It's too deep to be at risk of making a mess, which just makes my hips rise in the water as I push in the dildo faster, twisting it until I feel myself graze a sensitive spot. I clench down on it with a little moan, wishing I had a vibrator, but I left them all in my room in the apartment. They've been my only company for months — good purchases, but I've damn near destroyed the batteries on two.

Pulling the glass dildo out, I lift it from the water before muttering, "I need more. Screw this." I abandon the tub again, barely making it to the bed before I recline back on top of the duvet, legs spread. This time I let the dildo rock against my clit. The unforgiving hardness of the glass knocks against me, rubbing harshly as I rut my hips against it, then thrust it back into myself. The cycle repeats, each time I feel myself clenching, my breathing speeding up, I pull it out and rub my clit with it.

Finally I thrust it back in and hold onto the base, fucking myself fast with my hand, pushing deeper each time. The wet sounds that my sodden pussy makes send a shiver up my spine as I finally contract around the dildo, coming with a muffled shout around it. The glass slips free, landing on the bed as I shiver for a moment, convulsing as it feels like the entire house trembles.

When I come back to my senses, I realize the house *is* shaking.

Adrenaline has me out of the bed in seconds. I grab a fluffy robe and throw it on, taking the stairs two at a time as I reach the passageway, seeing smoke traveling up the stairs. I run down the stone steps barefoot, clad in only the bathrobe and my disc on my neck. When I reach the hoard, I stop short.

Reyes's dragon form is on his side, underbelly exposed as he breathes hard, filling the room with smoke. I don't have to guess what is wrong, because the slit between his hind legs is wide open, allowing his thick, scaled cock out to rest against his belly. Wet patches cover where his cock slides against him as his body shudders once.

My mouth drops open as I watch one of his upper arms shift, pressing his cock against his belly as he rubs himself. More pre-cum spills from the tapered tip until he snarls, his head swiveling.

Bright gold eyes stare me down, the inverse of how they were six months ago. This time his slitted iris is the only black in his golden gaze, far more alert than before. His mouth opens and hot breath mixed with smoke exhales as his entire body shivers. "*Maisie...*"

God, his voice. It's so deep, rough from disuse, sending shivers up my spine as I step onto the gold. His eyes lock on me as he bares his fangs. I freeze, holding the robe close.

"*Take it off.*" He snarls the words, staring at the robe. "*Nothing covers what is mine.*"

The implication catches me off guard as we stare at each other. I reach up, pushing it off my shoulders and leaving it on the stone as I step back onto the piles of gold, bare naked. His eyes slit, more smoke leaving his nostrils as he hums, the growl reverberating through the cavern as he licks his lips.

"*Let me make this slightly easier.*" His entire body shivers, then begins to shrink. He manages to get to a size closer to an orc, or other larger species, covered head to toe in his black scales, his horns twisting on his head as he rolls his neck. Reyes stands on top of the gold pile entirely naked, a thick tail coiling around his legs as his clawed fingers and toes flex. He's like a human dripped in the skin of a dragon and I walk toward him like I'm in a trance.

The moment I'm close enough, Reyes pulls me close and cups my face, kissing me with an open mouth. It's hot — literally — his skin is almost burning as he embraces me, his hands going down until he grasps my ass and pulls me flush against him.

"I heard you," he snarls, voice still husky from disuse. "You did so much while I was resting, thank you. Now let me return the favor." Reyes lifts me, then turns us both, pinning me against a pillar near the center of the room. My legs part as he drops a hand between my thighs and runs it over my slit. Two of his claws disappear with a little *snick* before he thrusts human-shaped fingers into me. They slide in like they were made for me, the scales on his skin only making the rough motion hotter as he fucks me quick and fast, kissing me senselessly.

I gasp against his lips, my hips rolling down instinctively. He breathes out against my throat, filling the air with smoke between us. With one hand, I hold onto the base of one of his horns, crying out as his fingers curl, rubbing that sensitive spot again.

"That's it, treasure. Come for me."

The orgasm that hits makes my thighs shake as I tremble between his body and the pillar. Reyes smiles slowly, his eyes flickering over my face with a satisfied look. "So quick. You were ready for that one. And you look beautiful with only my gold on."

I flush, opening my mouth as his fingers slip out. "I shouldn't have—"

"No," he growls, then he bites at my jaw in reprimand. "You deserve all the finest pleasures, including orgasms that make you shiver and leak all over everything I own. I've waited almost five centuries for you."

My heart stops as I look up at him. "What?"

"Dragons mate for life." He pulls his head back, eyes narrowing. "Though it's uncertain when that life will begin. I had to wait for you. I paid witches and warlocks to divine my future. I paid sirens to tell me where I could find my deepest desire, and when a siren finally took pity on me and divined the exact way I would find you, I put out the ad. Because I knew there had to be a catch — and it was to meet you so briefly, in my worst state, and trust that you were the one as I went to rest. When you were the only one who replied, I knew the siren was truthful. *You* bear my gold. *You* took care of me while I slept. It can be no one else." Reyes tilts his chin toward my throat. "Every time you came, I felt it. My gold on you was a bridge between us while I slept."

Every time I fucked myself at the apartment in the last six months flashes through my mind as I feel my cheeks flame with heat. "*Oh*."

Reyes smiles. "You like to get off, don't you, treasure? Work hard, but play harder." He hums, deep in his chest. One claw pulls at my lower lip and I open my mouth as he slips it inside. My tongue curls around it as I suck on his finger.

His eyes are hooded as I feel his tail wrap around a thigh, pulling me open wider. "Any qualms about me fucking you in my hoard, Maisie? I want my gold dripping with you."

With him pressed against me, I can't think of a single reason *why* I wouldn't want him at this very moment. Every weird occurrence in the past almost six months makes sense, including Faenir's insistence that I don't need an assistant of my own.

That bastard knew all along.

"Fuck me." I pull him back to me, kissing him hard as he tugs me away from the pillar briefly. His wings flare out, just as wide as before, but the leather is softer and tipped with feathers. It's like the rest allowed him to shed his old skin. They beat once, then twice, before we're in the air. My stomach swoops as he holds onto me, pushing my hips against his. His cock slides against me, thicker in this form, but not impossible like his fully shifted dragon.

Reyes kisses me as his tail helps to hold me mid-air as we line up. Reaching a hand between us, I grab onto him as one of his hands grazes my chest. Hiccuping back a moan, I notch him at my entrance, breathing out as he takes me in a single thrust. "A perfect fit," Reyes snarls in my ear, making me shiver as he starts to pump his hips, the beating of his wings matching the pace of my heart.

The tip of his tail slips between us, flickering back and forth on top of my clit in light teases as his head drops. He lavishes my breasts, groaning as his hips pump faster. "Such a sweet body, so soft. You've eaten well while I've rested and taken care of yourself." He groans, pushing deeper into me. "Do you like spending my gold, treasure? Because it makes me hard knowing you could drain both my balls and my bank accounts dry. I may have collected these pieces all myself, but it was for *you*."

I convulse around him, shuddering in his arms as I cry out, feeling him pound into me deeper. My head hangs back as his tail rubs against my clit. His voice in my ear, rasping about how much he wants me to use up everything he's ever gathered makes me spasm around him. His cock jerks and I feel a warmth as he grunts, rocking faster. Claws dig into my ass as he supports my lower back, spreading my cheeks wide.

Suddenly, his tail moves from rubbing my clit to nudging at my ass. I let out a breath as it slips around the muscles, completely lost in the pleasure of him fucking me mid-air, thousands of pounds of shimmering gold underneath and around us. Just as his tail slips inside and begins to pump into me, he buries his teeth into my nipple.

I scream his name, shaking as I come around him, scrambling for purchase with one hand on his shoulder while my other grips a horn as hard as I can.

He laughs, loudly and wickedly as he keeps moving. "That was just the first. Come on, Maisie. Drench your dragon's cock with your cum, make sure anyone who scents me will only smell your mark on my scales."

He fucks me right into my fourth orgasm of the night. My body trembles in his arms as he holds me up, his tail fucking me in tandem with his thick cock that only seems to grow larger with each time I clench around him. I moan, slurring my words as I soak him again. "Too much — I — *Reyes* —"

His body shudders against mine as his wings tilt, gliding us back to the gold. It's only then that he pushes us both down, pinning me to the pile as his hips pump. His lips find mine, unyielding but kind as he breathes harder. "I know." He sounds slightly more human as he moans this time, fucking me in long, slow strokes. "One more and I'll fill you, treasure. Once more until I'm done this time and I'll shower you with anything you desire. Anything you could need or ever want is *yours*. I will give it to you." He cups my face, continuing to talk as the gold under us shifts and clinks.

My eyes roll into the back of my head as his tail stuffs me full, rubbing against his throbbing cock through the thin wall separating them. I give a broken cry as he hits deep inside me. Then Reyes is gasping against my lips as he suddenly pounds into me twice as fast as before, his body shaking over mine as his wings flex and tremble. His cock jerks once, then twice, rubbing against my g-spot before he empties inside me.

I take it with a loud scream, panting some combination of *yes* and *god* as I come around him so hard my thighs lock up. It pushes him slightly free, his tail slipping out of me as I writhe against the gold under us. My orgasm only finishes when he pulls out to just the tip, rocking it up against my inner walls until I squirt with a shuddered gasp. He gets what he wants, because our combined release drips down onto the treasure below us.

Reyes pants above me, a smile creeping across his face as he presses soft kisses over my pounding pulse. With gentle hands, he rubs my sides, making little shushing sounds. "I should have done a better job preparing you for this, but I was certain you'd decline the position if you knew my true intentions."

I feel brainless and boneless as I catch my breath. When he moves his forehead to press it against mine, I mutter, "You can't have all the deciding power back. I'm busy with projects."

Reyes laughs, the sound loud and barking as it echoes off the hoard of gold and the stone cavern walls. "I wouldn't dream of it. From what I've gleaned, you've fulfilled my role better than I ever did."

My eyes narrow as I pull him back into a kiss. "Damn right."

He cups my face sweetly, settling over me. The concept of being immediately claimed by him doesn't freak me out as much as it should. I've had almost half a year to adjust to his life *without* him, and now the concept of doing it with someone else beside me feels like I won the lottery. There's just...

"Who's Baoriec?"

Reyes pauses as he kisses across my cheeks, mapping my face with his lips. "The warlock I hired in 1875 to help me scry for your name. I used a combination of old magics and blood oaths to figure out who you were. When I learned I had to wait more than a hundred years, I lost it. He quit." Rolling his eyes, smoke puffs out from his human nostrils. "He acted like I was going to eat him. I haven't done that since the Crusades."

He kisses the tip of my nose, his lips twitching as he recites, "*Sweet spring treasure of new undergrowth, fall into my embrace for an eternal oath, winter berry stained kiss of paired souls, passing seasons with twisted ribbon maypoles, fair as summer sun, meant to be the one.*" The full poem, encompassing the entire changing of the seasons, makes my heart lurch as Reyes plants a sweet kiss to my lips.

"*My* one. *My* treasure."

I kiss him with my hands tangled in his soft hair. "My dragon. I hope you slept well."

"I will only sleep now when you're in the bed beside me." He smiles as he lifts me from the gold and walks across the shifting piles to the stone staircase. "Thank you for taking care of me, treasure. I'm rested, which means it's your turn."

As he carries me up the stairs, the disc bounces on my throat, warm to the touch as I rest a head on his shoulder, kissing the scales there.

This wasn't a random stroke of luck — it's my own fairy-tale ending.

ACKNOWLEDGMENTS

Thank you to Anne-Marie, Silvy, Katie, and Ash for early reading these pieces for me. And thank you to my lovely editor Kai who always fixes my mistakes and leaves the best reactions while doing it.

It can be difficult to be an indie author somedays. Thank you to the readers who consistently show up, regardless of what genre I put out in the world. I see you, I recognize your names, and I hope that this little dip into monster romance is as fun for you all as it is for me.

If you've made it this far and read this anthology cover to cover, you're a monster fucker now. Welcome to the club.

ALSO BY R. L. RANDOLPH

Golden Omegaverse

June's Duet

Gold Rush (#1)

Gold Mine (#2)

Final Girls

The Felling Cut (#1)

Little Delights: A Monster Romance Anthology

Volume One (contemporary)

More books coming soon

ABOUT THE AUTHOR

R. L. Randolph is a mildly feral human woman who just wants to write about people kissing for her day job. She lives near the mountains, but, ironically, has grass and tree mold allergies so she never leaves the house.

FOR MORE INFORMATION

You can follow her on Instagram @rlrandolph or join her reader Facebook group here. Links to bonus content can be found here on her carrd. To stay up to date you can subscribe to her author newsletter here.

amazon.com/author/rlrandolph
facebook.com/rlrandolph
instagram.com/rlrandolph
rlrandolph.substack.com

www.ingramcontent.com/pod-product-compliance
Lightning Source LLC
LaVergne TN
LVHW090516110826
845146LV00003B/878